Edited by Maggie Helwig

COMING ATTRACTIONS
98

This book was written and published with the assistance of the Canada Council, the Ontario Arts Council and others. We acknowledge the support of the Canada Council for the Arts and the Government of Canada through the Book Publishing Industry Development Program for our publishing activities.

Acknowledgements: "What We Are Left With" by Leona Theis first appeared in *Prairie Fire*.

ISBN 0 7780 1096 1 (hardcover)
ISBN 0 7780 1098 8 (softcover)

Cover art by Amedeo Modigliani
Book design by Michael Macklem

Printed in Canada

PUBLISHED IN CANADA BY OBERON PRESS

Contents

Leona Theis' story "What We Are Left With" is about several things—the wounds that life leaves with us, but also what we hang on to. Her character Lillian holds on to the possibility of a brief moment of commonality over tea. Her chance to continue an interrupted argument with her husband forms, however slight and troubled, a thread of communication.

Two stories, one by Theis and one by Gabriella Goliger, deal with the last moments of communication between a child and a dying parent. "Elsa focuses what attention she still has on the soothing cool line of water on her lips," writes Theis. And Goliger ends her story with Rachel silently imploring her father to let her bear witness at Auschwitz—"Surely he must hear."

Meanwhile, Darryl Whetter of Fredericton gives us Danny, who writes his strained messages of desire and sadness on his own skin in hives, and Auster, the "whole language specialist," lost in his inability to communicate with the woman he loves and who has left him.

These three writers are implicated in different ways in history. Goliger's stories are all haunted by the Holocaust. Theis' history seems milder, more domestic, yet still shadowed in the background by "the Russians and their nuclear testing." Whetter, who has perhaps the most contemporary sensitivity of the three, begins one story with an explanation that "Prince Edward Island is to be murdered by a footrace.... Geography is ending." And this can be separated neither from the family whose story he is telling nor from the larger events of the world.

But all three write of people struggling toward speech, toward communication. And finally, that is what this collection is about—our effort, too, to speak to you out there, to say, "Listen to these people. Let them leave something with you."

MAGGIE HELWIG

Contributions for *Coming Attractions* 99, published or unpublished, should be sent directly to Oberon Press at 400–350 Sparks Street, Ottawa, Ontario, KIR 7S8 before 31 January, 1999. All manuscripts should be accompanied by a stamped, self-addressed envelope.

LEONA THEIS

What We Are Left With

Two things stay with Lillian from the robbery night before last. One is the stitch that fear has left in her stomach. The other is the purple pressure mark on the skin below her temple. She had pressed her cheek hard into the kitchen floor almost from the moment they ordered her to lie down until they left. She had borrowed steadiness from the floor, had used it to link herself to Howard who lay a few feet away from her.

The pressure mark has faded a little by now. Lillian leans toward the mirror and spreads makeup over the bruise. The purple turns grey.

Her daughter Joanie's reflection appears behind her in the bathroom mirror. "Don't wear black, Mum," she says. "Wear something cheerful. Yellow or green."

As soon as Lillian called yesterday morning, Joanie had closed Crystal Health Foods, left little Matthew with her roommate Carol, and driven over from Ripley. Howard doesn't want her here. Told Lillian he could do without her quackery, her New Age hocus pocus. Today, at Joanie's insistence, they will have a ceremony for the dog the robbers killed. She wants to free his soul, she says.

The linoleum, cool and steady against Lillian's cheek the night before last. The smell of Mr. Clean because she'd mopped up before they drove into town for Norm and Jean's anniversary party. Old linoleum, laid in 1965 when Joanie was learning to walk. Little baby shoes stepping over its printed roses and branches, scuffed patches on her white toes from all the early missteps.

Now a big black shoe, almost a boot—with yellow stitches all around where the upper meets the sole—is planted by the table leg. The girl wearing the boots half-sits on the table, half-leans against it. Her other foot swings back and forth above the floor. Lillian cannot guess at what makes this girl with long brown hair and freckles like spilled cinnamon take to carrying a tire wrench. Or what makes this boy listen to her orders. These two are from some foreign world. You can't get there from here.

They are little more than children really, these two who now tramp through the house and who have told them to lie down facing in different directions. Lillian cannot see Howard. She tries to send the memory of Joanie's white baby shoes to him through the floor. Wants to give him something to fill his mind and replace what is happening this moment. She raises her head to turn toward him.

"Don't move," the girl says. Barks. The way Pepper does when a stranger drives into the yard. There was no greeting from Pepper when Lillian and Howard drove up tonight. No damp nose breathing clouds onto the black vinyl of her purse, no front paws snagging her slacks. The farmyard so oddly quiet, the light from the living-room windows throwing rectangles on the snow-dusted dogwoods and peonies. Howard and Lillian made for the house without a thought about danger because, even in their imaginations and even though there was no sign of Pepper, there would never be someone in their house who had no right to be there.

Lillian obeys the girl's command, presses her cheekbone down again. It is better after all not to meet Howard's eyes. If this is the end then some things are better left unsaid. If not, there will be plenty of time to talk. Plenty of reason as well. Howard had no right to stand in front of a dozen people at the party for Norman and Jean's fortieth and declare that his daughter makes her living by stealing from people who don't know any better. Tricking them into paying good money in exchange for oily-looking pills and flavourless crackers.

But there may never be a chance to talk about that. Whatever this young girl and young boy plan to do to

11

them, they will do. Lillian only hopes it won't hurt too much or too long. She's ready enough for the end, but she isn't ready for it to hurt.

"Goddam you're slow!" the girl shouts up the stairs to her partner. "Get down here."

A series of muffled bumps and curses and the boy stumbles down the stairs, through the hall, into the kitchen, dragging a green garbage bag.

"So. What you got?" the girl asks him. Accuses him.

"Got a loonie collection," the boy says. His voice is surprisingly deep for someone so young but it cuts in and out like a radio with a loose wire. "And some stamps. Quite a few. Some necklaces and earrings and stuff."

"Stamps! What am I supposed to do with stamps? Not worth the space they take up in the bag. And a bunch of junk jewellery. This place doesn't have shit worth stealing. You don't have *shit* worth stealing!" she yells at the floor, at Howard, at Lillian.

So they have emptied Lillian's trinket box. The girl is right; they won't find anything they can get money for. Howard has never bought jewellery for her, isn't good at gift-giving at all for that matter, doesn't know how to buy pretty presents, women's comforts, sweet-smelling soaps and oils. Mostly he doesn't try. Sticks to kitchen gadgets. One Christmas—years ago—he'd gone out on a limb and bought her talcum powder. A big red shaker full of Old Spice brand. Didn't appear to know Old Spice was for men.

"That's the right stuff, isn't it? I got a feeling from the store lady I maybe bought the wrong thing."

"It's fine, Howard. It's fine."

Joanie, a teenager at the time, shifted beside Lillian on the sofa, shook her head, snatched the wrapping-paper, squashed it into a ball. Threw it down and stomped off and shut herself in the bathroom.

"For after your bath, right?" Howard said to Lillian. "For your skin?"

"For after my bath."

Suppose these robber children just leave them alone now, run away with their garbage bags full of worthless loot. Suppose she and Howard do not die here on the floor without ever looking at each other again. Suppose they go on for years? Housecleaning on Mondays, card game in town on Wednesdays, pub on Fridays, Church on Sundays. Joanie checking in by phone every weekend. Howard waving away the receiver in Lillian's hand. Then surely they will have to finish the argument they were in the middle of when they drove up and saw the light shining from the windows and felt the quiet in the yard.

"Christ! The old man's up and croaked on us Gertie!" The boy's radio voice cuts in and out. "He's kicked it!"

Oh Jesus, Oh Jesus. Lillian feels a rush of terror and soaks her slacks.

"No he didn't," the girl says, calm as can be. "He's fainted stupid. Seen it before."

"How do you know, Gertie? How do you know?"

"I said I seen it before," the girl says and her voice gets louder. "Seen it lots."

The girl walks over to where Howard lies. Her tread depresses the floor slightly, easing the pressure against Lillian's cheekbone for an instant with each step.

Maybe the girl wants to see for herself if Howard is dead. Maybe she will hold her finger under his nose to feel for breath. Maybe she just wants to pick up the wallet she told Howard to pull out of his pocket before he lay down. Lillian thinks of the tire wrench on the table and doesn't try to look at Howard or the girl.

After a moment the steps come closer to where Lillian lies. "Old lady's pissed her pants," the girl says. Lillian feels her muscles give again, feels her pants soak a little more. She clenches down there the way she used to for exercises after Joanie was born. Holds tight to steady every part of her insides. The muscles aren't as strong as she wants them to be.

The big black shoes walk over to the stove. Soon Lillian feels a tiny breeze and something flimsy settles over her backside. It's the tea-towel she keeps tucked through the oven door-handle.

"You don't like something, cover it up," the girl says. Lillian is glad of the towel. "Go get the VCR," the girl tells her partner.

"Now," she says, and her voice comes close to Lillian's ear. "Where the fuck's the good stuff?"

Joanie used to swear too. Went through a swearing phase that lasted years.

"There is none," Lillian says to the black shoe in front of her face. How does she know the shoe won't swing into her nose any second?

Joanie had opened her present that Christmas, the talcum powder Christmas, and said, "I'm supposed to wear something you bought in Ripley at Wilson's f-ing *dime* store to school?" Lillian cannot even think the swear word inside her head. "It isn't enough that my parents are *ancient*," Joanie had said. "That they look like the fortrel *twins* for Christ's sake. Now *I'm* supposed to wear a Wilson's f-ing *sweater*?"

But Joanie cleaned her mouth up somewhere along the line. Joanie never went around terrorizing seniors. Joanie grew up and learned how to support herself properly—after the first few missteps. Joanie does just fine in spite of what Howard says.

She has always been one surprise after another, Joanie has, starting with her appearance when Howard and Lillian were both almost 30 and thought children weren't going to come at all since they hadn't come yet. Then turning out to be smart as a whip but ignoring school in favour of boys by the time she was ten, and in favour of beer by the time she was fifteen. Running away in the middle of Grade 11 to live with her wild cousins in Regina. Suddenly settling down five years ago over in Ripley and having her own child. Refusing to say who the father is.

"Useless," the girl says to her partner. "Let's get the hell out of here."

Lillian is relieved and afraid. Relieved this will be over soon. Afraid they will hurt her. Afraid she will find out Howard is dead. Her ears hurt, as they often do. The ears are the children of the kidneys, Joanie has told her. The emotion associated with the kidneys is fear. Lillian has given in and agreed to let Joanie put her on a regime of special tea and tiny green pills for her ears.

Lillian closes her eyes. The floor shudders as the girl and the boy run outside and down the steps and away without closing the door. Cold air rushes in and settles around her. She hears a vehicle start behind the house. It sounds like a half-ton. She doesn't get up until it is well out of the yard.

Lillian finishes her makeup and changes into a green dress for Joanie. She comes downstairs and the three of them wait a few minutes in the living-room. They look at their laps. They look out the window toward the shed. They look at each other. Howard's eyes are swollen, the way they have been for months. Lillian sees the grit in them each morning as if the sandman has stayed all night.

Joanie tried a few weeks ago to convince Howard to forgo his trip to the Flat Hill bar on Friday nights. The eyes are the children of the liver, she warned him. She wanted him to drink a tea that would clean him from the inside out. "You will see better," she said. Joanie doesn't know that Howard has a few beer on Tuesday nights too, sometimes on Wednesdays as well, and there's a bottle of whisky in the cupboard beside the television for when there's a game worth watching.

Howard refused to drink Joanie's tea. Instead he yelled

about her crazy ideas and asked if she wasn't embarrassed to be spouting that crap. He shouted that she's making fools of her parents, that people ask him at the pub about his New Age daughter.

"'Has she met Shirley MacLaine yet?' they ask me! They know all about that stuff, they read magazines. They know wacky when they see it. They laugh at you. At me. They ask me if you're going to find yourself a husband in a bottle of magic pills."

Joanie blurted that the emotion associated with the liver is anger. Howard left the room.

Today Howard wears his coveralls and his frayed work jacket. He is only there to do the heavy work, to do what's required he says. Not to be part of no funeral for no damn animal spirit.

Lillian will wait until after Joanie leaves to talk to him about Tuesday night. It isn't the robbery that she wants to talk about, they've been all through that with the Mounties. Those two won't get far, the Mounties say. Amateurs. They've hit three houses and everyone knows what they look like.

No, Lillian wants to finish the argument the robbery interrupted.

She knows nothing is about to change between Howard and Joanie even though they have been almost civil for the better part of two days. Nor between herself and Howard, in spite of the fright that is still with them. They will argue this latest thing through as they always do. And when they are done arguing their life will be the same mix of irritation and anger and public embarrassment it has been for years. The same mix of certainty and shared small rituals and the little ripple she still feels inside when he comes up behind her at the sink and lifts her hair as if they are still young. Lays his cheek against her neck the way he did at the Legion Hall in 1954 when she was a bridesmaid in marigold tulle and he was the best man.

Snow crunches underfoot as the three of them walk across the farmyard. Howard has dug the hole behind the old machinery shed. He had to keep a bonfire going for two hours yesterday to thaw the ground enough to dig. Now he drags the bulky tarp, with the rigid weight inside it, around the corner of the shed. Joanie bends to pull the tarp away. Howard stops her.

"Leave it," he says. "No need to look. We'll bury him like this."

Joanie steps back, looks steadily at the tarp, as if she can see Pepper's body by staring through the oiled canvas.

Howard uses his foot to nudge the body in its makeshift shroud gently into the hole. It is an awkward fit, the corpse frozen, the tarp stiff. He uses the shovel as a lever against the rim of the short grave to adjust first one end of the rigid bundle, then the other.

Lillian watches Joanie, who fixes her father now with the same hard stare she directed toward the tarp a moment ago. Lillian sets her mouth against the cold and the sore at the corner of her lip burns. Joanie has supplied her with two-tone red capsules to treat the sore. The mouth is the child of the heart. The capsules taste like plastic on Lillian's tongue but she takes one every day because who knows, maybe it will help. As she waits for Howard to fill the grave in, she thinks of the hot tea she will make when they go back to the house. Real tea, orange pekoe, for Howard and Lillian; something else for Joanie if she insists. Cold fingers wrapped around warm cups to feel the heat.

Passing On

Elsa was eight years old when Aunt Eleanor showed her what faith was about.

"Auntie, the others won't come to play anymore because of the bees' nest by the fence."

"Then we will remove the bees' nest."

Elsa watched as her aunt lifted the skirt of her long house dress clear of her sturdy, honest knees, knelt on the painted verandah boards, and petitioned God to keep her safe. Then Aunt Eleanor rose, walked directly down the back path, detached the remarkably quiet hive, and carried it calmly into the woods beyond.

That was 60 years ago.

Elsa can hardly hold herself back now that her daughter Judith has finally come. They need to talk things over. Talk many things over. "Sit down, sit down, dear," Elsa says and points an unsteady finger toward the yellow vinyl chair by the window that looks out onto the back lawn of the hospital. Judith sits.

"Is your teacher's convention done with, then?" Elsa asks, or thinks she asks. No response. Maybe Elsa is forgetting to say things out loud again. The nurses say she does that. ("You didn't *tell* me you needed the bathroom." "You didn't *say* to pull the curtains." *Yes I did. Three times I did.*)

She tries again, tries with something else. "There's so much I want to talk to you about. From the beginning on down. I want you to tell me everything you wish had been different."

This time Judith responds. "Just like that?" she says. "As if we're talking about something we can change, like the colour of the curtains?" Judith's tone is not particularly sarcastic; but she doesn't smile to take the edge off what she says either.

Elsa changes direction. "Did I ever tell you about your Great Aunt Eleanor?" she asks.

"Many times. You talked about her yesterday."

Yesterday. Judith was here yesterday and Elsa has forgotten. Must keep better track. Pay attention.

"Aunt Eleanor was a woman, Judith, who believed in possibilities. And in herself," Elsa says. "She was a woman who didn't give up easily. Aunt Eleanor told me I had persistence built into my nature because my last name was Will. Used to be Will. Before it was Eriksen." Elsa closes her eyes. She can see so much more when she closes her eyes, can call up the deep green of her aunt's dress, call up the sincerity in her face, call up whatever she wishes, without the pastel details of the hospital room in the way.

"You look tired, Mum," Judith says. "Just rest."

"But you're here now. We should talk."

"I'll be here later too."

Elsa Eriksen, née Will, was 25 and pregnant for the first time when Nels came home and told her he was out of a job. It was 1949. She heard him—earlier than he should be home—come up the outside stairs to their apartment. Heard him pause at the landing. He came in and hung his hat behind the door. Said he wouldn't be going to the railway yards any more. They'd let him go because the foreman caught him drinking in a box car, and not even on a break. Rye whisky from a mickey Young Carl carried around in the big front pocket of his overalls. So Young Carl was out of a job too, but he hadn't started a family yet—lived with his parents still. Carl was not in dire straits.

Nels sat down in his regular chair, the one they had to shift out of the way whenever Elsa needed to get at the pots in the bottom cupboard. "It's a real piece of bad luck," he said. But he'd always had good luck until this, he reminded her, and he'd be lucky again. Elsa felt compelled to go outside, where there would be more room for the huge piece of news Nels had brought home. She picked up the slop pail and edged around Nels. Pregnancy hadn't made her cut back on the amount of lifting she did. The water slapped back and forth inside the pail's thin lips but didn't spill. Elsa went out the door, down the stairs, across the dirt and dandelions. She tipped the slops into the trough at the back of the yard and watched as what didn't sink in right away ran into the back alley, leaving a bubble scum on the gravel.

She rubbed the soft little rise in her abdomen and said out loud, "We will all be fine." Fine because, in spite of this latest, Nels was a good worker. More honest than some. Hadn't tried to hide what happened, had he? Other men did things like this all the time. Nels had the bad luck to be caught, that was all.

The job wasn't the only thing, Elsa had to admit. Marriage hadn't changed Nels the way she'd hoped it would. He refused to see a dentist about his loosening teeth; he had a habit of wearing long-sleeved underwear with short-sleeved shirts and seemed not to realize how unkempt this made him look; he smoked so many cigarettes the lock of hair that hung over his forehead had a streak of yellow. The two of them couldn't seem to get through a week without shouting at each other. But that wouldn't go on.

Elsa wrote to her sister, "He's always kept a roof over our heads, Pauline. He's looking into new business opportunities."

Her letter showed the same stubborn faith, fastened way back to Aunt Eleanor's simple demonstration, that had seen Elsa through so far. Through the endless stretch of high school as it became clear she couldn't blame her lack of friends on a bees' nest in the back yard—people just did not gravitate toward her. Girls didn't ask her along when they went to the drugstore hoping to see the pharmacist's son James at the counter. James with his orderly teeth and his shiny black hair with the wave that stood up so dramatically above his forehead. Nor did her classmates invite her to sit with them in upstairs bedrooms and shape each other's hair into finger rolls before a big night out. Young men were polite but paid little attention to her. A fellow would dance with Elsa only if the partner he'd crossed the floor to ask was scooped away in front of him and Elsa stood so close it would be just too rude to walk past her.

Elsa knew how things stood. Nevertheless, she wrote down the details of every dance she did have and some that she didn't. The entries in her diary blended fact and fiction in a way that Elsa herself sometimes couldn't sort out. After her father left the household she wrote about him as though his absence was only temporary: "Dad will be so pleased to see how well the garden is doing." And, "I've organized the tool shed so Dad will have everything within easy reach. It's never been so orderly."

During the times when she had no address for her father, Elsa composed letters to him directly into her notebook. Hopeful letters. News of her mother, her sister Pauline, her younger brother Frederick. News of the library job she had convinced the Town Council to create for her. She listed for her father the speedy engagements and weddings among her contemporaries as local boys signed up for the air force and the army and prepared to leave. She wrote that she was looking forward to seeing him back home as soon as his finances improved—which they surely would any day. She expressed this last sentiment to Pauline.

You have quite an imagination, her sister said.

David Will had closed his insurance office in Bridgewater in 1937. His desk had collected more dust than business for three years before that. He worked his way through the rest of the depression with longer and longer stretches of odd jobs away from home. He picked up intermittent work at insurance offices in the cities and larger towns— answering letters, clerking. Talked his way in the door on the basis of what he knew about the business. It wasn't reliable work, it didn't pay well, and the checks he sent home were sporadic.

Elsa thought of her father as her real friend in the family. Her sister Pauline, her brother Frederick both seemed so young, and her mother didn't invite confidences. Elsa kept company with her journal and her embroidery, her novels and poetry anthologies. She quietly saved her money and ordered silver birch china by mail from Eaton's, one or two pieces at a time, for her hope chest. She spent two years optimistically waiting for attention from an Englishman who walked her home one evening after she closed the library.

She wrote: "John Jacobs accompanied me home. I had a sudden wish to walk the hills and footpaths of England with just such an amusing, reliable companion." Her fanciful nature compressed half a courtship into that single evening. Before she put her notebook away she wrote, "He told me I had a good gait."

John Jacobs had lived all his life on the Canadian prairies, but both his parents had grown up in England. To Elsa, this heritage implied a certain set of traits that had to do with education, afternoon tea, manners, and something less tangible that Elsa thought of as decency. In the local militia regiment, John Jacobs was an important man. He was also a teacher, as his father had been, and one of her most regular patrons at the library. She watched to see what books he borrowed—Rudyard Kipling, John Buchan's many novels, new British Penguin editions by almost anyone. Elsa added the titles to her own reading list.

On Sunday mornings when the rest of her family went to the unadorned, white Presbyterian Church, Elsa walked across town to the unfamiliar Anglican Church with the brown brick steeple. She went partly because she wanted to know that aspect of her Englishman's life, and partly for the opportunity simply to be in the same room as him. She sat in the last pew and watched so she would know when to kneel. John was tall, his shoulder so high it was level with the deep green netting that stood away from his mother's felt hat, the two of them up near the front in the same pew every Sunday. A small, proper family. On the rare occasions when John Jacobs' head turned and his eyes ran past Elsa sitting at the back of his church, she read a greeting in his expression.

Even after he stopped turning his head she kept on attending for a month. Finally Elsa had to admit that what she had insisted to herself was special attention was really only courtesy, and even the courtesy was growing more dilute with each visit John Jacobs made to the library. She wrote him out of her diary and moved her optimism to someone new. Nels Eriksen was a solid-looking Norwegian with early wrinkles in his leathery face, a back that was broader than the Englishman's, and a set of seasoned workboots. He had built the fires for her in the library through two winters. At the end of the second spring he asked her if just anyone could borrow things to read. He took home back copies of *Popular Mechanics* two at a time.

Nels was a Reserve man too, the same regiment as John. He had a slight limp and a chronically ill father. Elsa guessed that it was one or the other of these that kept him on this side of the Atlantic. The relationship developed slowly, sometimes seeming as if it was not a relationship so much as an assumption between them. Nels still lived with his mother and father on a farm at the edge of town. The running of the farm was up to him, and he would not shut it down, would not entertain notions of change, while his father was still alive. Old Olaf died in 1945. Nels and his mother ran the place for another year before they rented the land out and bought a house in town.

The war had been over for almost three years when Elsa and Nels married. They moved to Flat Hill for the CPR job and took the apartment over the post office. Elsa had her very own home to keep. She left most of her books stored in her mother's attic in Bridgewater. The few she took with her stayed packed in their moving-day box, along with her own journals, underneath the bed in the apartment.

Elsa knew how to be frugal. When the pair of old sheets her mother gave her "for starting out" wore in the centre, she split them and turned them to, so that she and Nels slept with a seam down the middle of the double bed. She grew fewer irises than her mother had, used most of her patch in the landlord's yard for carrots and potatoes, for peas and beans and beets that she canned in the fall. Elsa regularly carted Nels' overalls down the street to mend the knees on Isabelle Hepburn's Singer; the crochet hooks Aunt Eleanor gave her stayed folded away in paper. She read less than she liked, but Elsa was fond of the poetry of her new name, the way its syllables rolled up and down. Elsa Eriksen.

Nels' mother came to visit, clattered up the outside stairs and into Elsa's kitchen carrying enamelled tubs and heavy cast-iron pans. Cooking lessons. Elsa was introduced to foods her own mother had never even been in the same room with. She learned to soak the *lutefisk* overnight before she baked it at Christmas time, to take out the strong lye taste. She learned to bring it to the table with butter so hot it ran like whisky. She learned to stop imagining a sharp pain in her front teeth every time she saw Nels sip his tea through a spoonful of sugar.

"We need to find someone who will carve you a rolling-pin," Nels' mother said. "You can't make proper *lefse* without a fluted rolling-pin. See, thin and strong like a linen napkin is how the dough should be when you're through with it."

Losing the railway job had been a setback, no question, but Nels had been on steady as a welder at Brackman's three months to the day when Judith was born. It was long enough to recover, almost, from the stretch when they'd been on relief, although they still owed two months' back rent.

Elsa's water broke just as she brought Nels' spare overalls in from the clothesline. She stood a moment in the kitchen, feeling the stream turn from warm to cold on her legs, checking the stitching on the long patches she'd sewn inside the thighs of Nels' pants to line the scattered burn holes the welding sparks left. He'd grunted and thrown them on the table without a word the last time a patch had come away. Elsa left a note on the kitchen table to tell Nels where she was, put on a coat to hide where the wet made her dress turn dark, and walked two blocks to the cottage hospital. By the time she arrived, she was bent low with back labour.

It was small and homey, the cottage hospital—well-named—the smell of medical clean buffered by the gentle scent of baby powder.

University Hospital, where Elsa is now, bears little resemblance to the old cottage hospital back home. It helps Elsa sort out the two, the fact that they're so different. She knows just where she is, most of the time. She opens her eyes and sees white gloss paint on the ceiling. Her gut hurts as if tiny creatures inside scrape at the walls. She raises herself on one elbow and tries to guess the time of day from the light and shadow in the room. Afternoon?

There's Judith, asleep in the chair beside the window. It's good she has finally come. There's so much to talk about when she wakes up.

Elsa knows enough about Judith's current troubles to guess at how things are in the schools these days. Students out of control. Parents on your back about every little thing. Judith says all her energy goes to what she calls classroom management, nothing left for teaching. Elsa wants Judith to know there will come a day when everything that makes her anxious now will seem far, far away. But there's no use saying that to someone who's right in the thick of things.

Suddenly Judith is right there beside the bed. "What is it Mum? I didn't hear what you said. Can I get you something?"

"Just thinking out loud," Elsa says. She must have been doing just that. Judith's voice brings her back in touch with the real and the physical, including the real, physical pain she's been trying to ignore. There is no question she's dying. The cancer must be everywhere inside. Perhaps a doctor has even told her so, she can't remember. It hardly matters what doctors say at this point, because Elsa herself is certain. Her imminent death is one reason Judith is here with her. They don't normally see much of each other. All the more reason to talk now. Concentrate. Get to the point.

"How was your teachers' convention?" Elsa says.

"Not so great. People listening to themselves talk."

Elsa closes her eyes but stays in the conversation. "Do you still want to quit teaching?"

"I don't think that's a choice I have. No fall-back position. No partner either."

"Sometimes a husband is no help anyway—certainly your father wasn't much help."

"So you've told me. More than once." Judith says. "We don't need to go into all that again."

"Would you rather talk about this?" Elsa lifts her arms a few inches off the bed and gestures feebly at the air, as if by doing so she can describe the room, the bed, her body on the bed, the reason they are in this particular place together. "Because *I* would rather not," Elsa says. "Feels like an excavation going on inside me."

"I'm sorry," Judith says. "But I already know how things were. I don't need to go mucking through history all over again. And I can't understand why *you* want to talk about it. You were always so...mad all the time."

Elsa opens her eyes and looks at Judith. Looks and listens. She doubts her daughter would believe her if she tried

26

to tell her how all that anger has thinned out. Evaporated into little patches. It's evaporating still.

Her daughter shrugs. "It's what I remember," Judith says. "You mad at Dad. You mad at the town. You mad at anyone who had better luck than we had."

This is true. Elsa must have been about the same age Judith is now when she stood on the Church steps after the service and told Reverend Moore that faith is only good so far as it goes—there are some things it just isn't equal to. And maybe even younger when Elsa called her sister Pauline just to say that even a strong last name like Will couldn't keep a person going forever. Judith probably heard both those conversations. Likely remembers them.

"I can't use up our little bit of time making sense out of all that for you," Elsa says. Her whole set of old grudges has shrunk. Anger seems less important all the time. Some memories are still sharp when they surface, but they grow dull with exposure.

The dozen small pointed blades that have been stabbing Elsa from the inside merge into a single keen sword. She draws a sudden breath, squeezes Judith's hand. Judith pushes the button for the nurse.

The whistle of the one o'clock train vibrated through the dark house like a blue note. Elsa sat at the kitchen table, the baby sweat-warm against the front of her nightie. The train sounds sent a shiver across her back. She nursed Judith in the kitchen at night, so as not to disturb Nels' sleep. She wondered who would be down at the rail yards with the train. Not Young Carl. She'd seen him go by on his way to the station just after lunch. He'd be home by now. Carl had talked his way back on with the boss within a month of being let go for drinking. They'd checked his pockets for the clink of glass every day for the first two weeks, he'd told Nels and Elsa, then left him alone. Why don't you come back too? he'd said. But when Nels went by, hearing they needed help coopering grain cars, the station agent told him he had a full crew. Lucky bugger, Nels said about Carl, crediting the difference between their two situations to nothing more predictable than a throw of the dice.

Judith fell asleep at the breast. Elsa ran her finger around the ring Nels' whisky glass had left on the table. She licked her finger to wet it, traced the ring again, and licked a second time. Her tongue puckered.

The next morning Elsa told Nels she didn't want him to drink in the house anymore. The whisky bottle, still with two inches of amber in the bottom, went into the fridge and stayed there. Nels followed to the letter her request not to drink at home. The hotel was a ten-minute walk from the house. By law, the beverage room closed between six and seven. Weeknights, Nels arrived home at ten past six for supper and left again at ten minutes to seven. Elsa poured her family into this small reservoir of time. She recounted Judith's latest accomplishments to Nels, talked about her daily round of errands, coaxed him for conversation about work. She painted the little wooden corner cupboard yellow for Judith to use when she played house. "See," she showed Nels when he came in. "I even did the shelf inside."

She wrote to Pauline: "He wants to make Judith a set of play dishes to put in her cupboard. He has me saving the lids of tobacco cans and peanut butter tins so he can paint them green."

Elsa waited three weeks before she painted the makeshift dishes herself. She was outside stirring turpentine into the paint with a scrap of wood split off the back fence when she saw Young Carl go by across the street. He was on his way to work, stride long, shoulders loose. The word was he'd made an offer on the empty McCallum house and everyone knew that charming Anna Spencer would say yes to him any day. Elsa stirred and stirred until the sharp-smelling turpentine blended with the paint in a thin, even mixture.

When her second pregnancy miscarried on the same day Aunt Eleanor died, Elsa felt everything behind and in front of her buckle and shake. There was a fight the night before the funeral, as there had been the Sunday before and the Sunday before that. The rolling-pin that Nels' Uncle Herman had carved—the one with the hard ridges for making *lefse*—made a dent in the plaster in the kitchen wall. Elsa was never clear afterward if the dent happened when Nels threw the rolling-pin at her or when she threw it at him. Nor could she say who threw first. What stayed with her afterward was the picture of little Judith scrambling in and out amongst their feet. Screaming. Crawling under the kitchen table to hide. Elsa wanted to quiet her somehow—wrap her small shoulders in a blanket, brush the hair back gently from her forehead—but the greedy roar inside her own head swiped away her best intentions.

It was a question of pacing, Elsa concluded. She could give Judith a decent start as long as she could stretch her own energy across a known time frame. An article in *McCall's* said that if you can get a child safely through to age three or four then the pattern will be set. Your child will always know who she is and who loves her, and that will carry her through anything. Elsa resolved to hold herself together until Judith's fourth birthday.

The shouting and shoving between Elsa and Nels continued and Judith still screamed in the centre of it, but Elsa made it her job to manufacture security through little acts of will. She stuck to firm routines, listened when she hardly cared to, pretended delight at Judith's drawings, gave her elementary cooking lessons—breaking eggs, stirring pancakes. She ordered herself to make sure there was a story, a kiss and a bedtime prayer every night. As soon as Judith learned to count well enough, they played games together from the cardboard chest *Ten Games for Children* that Judith's Grandma Will sent one year for Christmas. Steeplechase and Parcheesi. Snakes and ladders, which made Judith impatient and which Elsa told her was about persistence, about keeping on.

The house Nels had put the down payment on before she lost the second baby was bigger by half than the apartment, and Elsa moved her things into the tiny third bedroom. She did better than her promise to herself about Judith's fourth birthday. In fact, her daughter was almost nine by the time Elsa retreated to the point where she spent most of her time in her room. After that, though, she rarely came out when Nels was in the house, spoke to him only when necessary. She did what she had to do to keep things running: made sure Judith was fed; washed her clothes but didn't mend them; helped with homework when she could muster her resolve; tried to manufacture conversations with her daughter, but failed more often than not. Occasionally, Elsa even made it to Sunday service or to a meeting of the United Church Women, avoiding certain people and keeping up a thin connection with those who were kind enough to make small talk, tactful enough not to mention her irregular appearances.

The year Judith was eleven, Elsa's sister Pauline, whose husband had a good desk job with the Post Office in Bridgewater, supplied two yards of mint-green velvet and a packet of rick-rack to outfit her for the Explorer Girls' fashion show. Elsa made a rare excursion down the street with Judith in tow to put the dress together at Isabelle Hepburn's house. When she was finished she folded the leftover pieces and stored them in a corner of her own room where they were soon covered with piles of attendant mending and scraps intended for quilts.

There was a fight about the house. Elsa said the neighbours would complain soon about the peeling paint and the cardboard taped in the hall window if they didn't do something. And the mayor living just down the block. Nels said there was no money for paint and who had time to do it anyway? Elsa sat in her room with Judith's old box of wax crayons and drew pictures of houses. None of them looked at all like her own. She drew irises in front of the houses, tiger lilies, tulips. Then she left the houses out of the pictures completely and drew only flowers, big ones that filled the whole page. Some she drew by making patterns of little x-marks, so they looked crudely like the cross-stitch pictures she used to make before she married Nels. When Judith stopped in the doorway of Elsa's room and asked what she was doing, Elsa gave her a verbal lambasting and sent her away.

Elsa unpacked her old books and kept them close around herself in her room. Kipling, Housman, Buchan. *The Oxford Book of English Verse*. She liked the calm, matte feel of the Housman pages, was drawn to the tissue-thin leaves of the *Oxford*. Her mother supplied her each year at Christmas with subscriptions to the *Saturday Evening Post* and *McCall's*. Elsa tore the short stories from every issue and kept them laid flat in apple boxes. She packed a suitcase one Tuesday and wrote to Pauline that she'd be on the bus on Monday. Get away. Maybe for good. When Monday came she didn't make the bus, but she did make it out of the house.

She borrowed a doddering Smith-Corona from Reverend Moore, who had acquired a new typewriter and assured her there was no inconvenience. Three weeks of drill brought her typing speed back up to what it had been when she made book lists at the library. For practice she reproduced, word by word, entire chapters from Judith's copy of *Emily of New Moon*. She wrote imaginary letters to Aunt Eleanor. *Judith continues to do well in school. She is a favourite with the teachers. It is some trouble keeping her in clothes but Mum has knit her a new sweater, which helps. The house is very cold in this weather. Nels's work is steady still but his eyesight is deteriorating.*

Elsa searched out work in bits and pieces. She set up shop on the kitchen table during the day and did invoices for Morgan's farm equipment, shifting the carbon at intervals to keep it fresh, darting a hand up to flick the wire arm back into place every time the "t" stuck. She typed and retyped a thesis for a local farmer who grew special plots of seed during the summer and spent his winters off at the university. She paid off three months of past-due grocery bills; bought a piece of glass that she puttied into the hall window where the cardboard had been; learned to pass Nels in the kitchen without speaking at all. And she began to accept that Judith almost never spoke to her.

Elsa and Nels carried on their co-existence, sometimes flaring at each other, sometimes just stirring the coals. Elsa kept Reverend Moore's typewriter clattering in the background with one small job after another. Judith didn't scream anymore when her parents started up; she just left the house—late at night, early in the morning, Sunday afternoon. She must have had places to go.

"Where have you been?"

"Out. Around."

"Where did you sleep last night?"

"Donna's."

"You weren't with that Sonter boy were you?"

"No, I wasn't with that Sonter boy."

It might be true. It might not. "Next time tell me where you're going. You have to tell me where you're going."

"Right."

Light sears Elsa's eyes when she opens them. She closes her lids again quickly, then opens them just enough that she has a slit to look through. Something in the slant of the rays looks like late afternoon, early evening. This can't be right—she has always arranged things so that her bedroom window faces east. She squints across the room. Her window is the wrong shape. The curtains are no colour at all. The hospital. University Hospital. Judith is here. Has been here long enough to fall asleep in that awful moulded plastic chair. She looks so uncomfortable. If Elsa could move more easily she would find Judith a pillow, tuck a blanket around her shoulders. Rock her.

Elsa pulls herself out of bed, leans on the wheeled bed-side table, and uses it to walk herself over to the window. The noise wakes Judith. "Mum, you're up," she says, pushing her legs straight out in a stretch.

"Judith...."

"Yes Mum?"

"Thank you for coming, Judith."

"Of course Mum."

Elsa focuses on a water-damage mark on the window-sill. She concentrates on speaking out loud so Judith will hear her.

"Judith?"

"Yes." Judith comes to stand beside her, puts a hand lightly on her arm.

Elsa doesn't go on. Leaning on the unstable table makes breathing difficult. The table rolls ahead a touch and Elsa's legs begin to shake.

"Let me get you back into bed," Judith says.

"Judith...?" There is something else. She wants to talk to Judith about Aunt Eleanor, about faith, even, but she can't. Religion embarrasses her. She suspects any discussion of faith would embarrass Judith as well.

"Yes Mum?"

Elsa doesn't answer. Judith helps her back to the bed and settles her in.

"Do you want a drink? I'll get you some fresh water."

"This is good just like this," Elsa says. She closes her eyes. "This is good. ...Good to lie here quietly now." Maybe she'll try again to talk to Judith. A little later. It occurs to her that what she practices might have nothing to do with religion, with faith, the way other people think of it. Just some stubborn idea that she must keep at it. Whatever *it* might be. But maybe Judith doesn't need to talk about this. Maybe determination is built right into Judith's nature. At any rate, something has brought her this far.

"You're all right, aren't you Judith?" Elsa says. There is a short silence.

"I'm fine," Judith says. She pauses, then says, "Most of the time I'm fine. You sleep, Mum."

Unsteady hands adjust Elsa's blanket; she senses the fatigue in the hands. Judith will need a good rest after this many hours waiting in a hospital-room. Is it hours? Must be days. A good rest after this many days at the bedside.

Elsa's heard her daughter—she's almost certain—singing old lullabies beside her bed some time in the last few hours. And she's heard her reciting a children's prayer. Where she learned the lullabies heaven only knows. Elsa was never one to sing them. But didn't she hear a line or two from "All Through the Night" in Judith's unstable alto a minute ago? And the spoken words "Now I lay me down to sleep...," a phrase that can comfort even an atheist if she's repeated it often enough as a child. Can comfort against all odds, built as it is on the possibility of death each time you put your cheek on the pillow.

Judith must be as tired as tired. The girl needs rest. She doesn't need talk about aunts who died long ago, or how to find your way out of a low spot or about what you can learn from a game of snakes and ladders. She'll dredge up the details of the past and make her own sense of them in her own good time. The best thing Elsa can do for Judith now is to depart.

Her stomach feels a little better for the moment. They must have given her something easier to manage for lunch today. She sleeps. She wakes. The sheet feels heavier than cotton ought to feel. There's movement beside the bed. Someone settles her hair away from her forehead, wets her dry mouth with a swab. Elsa focuses what attention she still has on the soothing cool line of water on her lips.

34

Air Masses

It's hot, sweltering. It's been that way for days now, so hot the milk is turning sour, as if even the fridge isn't equal to the challenge. There was a storm last night. A tornado touched down east of the city; it flung buildings apart and pulled up trees and put them through a spin cycle. The temperature in the city dropped fifteen degrees in a single hour last night, but this morning the cement patio on the south side of the house was baking again by breakfast time. When Mellie went out to water the flowers this afternoon she turned the hose on the cement first to wet it down so she wouldn't scorch the soles of her bare feet.

Mellie's night-time dreams have multiplied, as they sometimes do in the heat. She dreamed her old dream of waking up in a department store wearing nothing but a mauve slip; and the other one where she was back in school writing exams for subjects she'd never studied. She dreamed of driving up a hill, a hill that became steeper and steeper as she climbed, the wheels lifting off when the grade finally became too abrupt; the car drifting backwards through still, quiet air in slow somersaults. Her stomach couldn't keep up with the motion.

Paul doesn't seem to understand about dreams of falling. And a dream about hills doesn't make sense for a girl from the prairies, he told her this morning. He must be unaware that it takes almost no effort of imagination to exaggerate a landscape—at night, in the dark, in a dream. And apparently he's forgotten about the hills hidden in the countryside back home. Not the low hummock close to the grain elevators that gave Flat Hill its name, it wasn't much of a hill—but the other ones, the ravines that took you by surprise on country roads; slopes that, instead of rising from the horizon, slid suddenly below it.

Mellie hardly knew Paul when they both lived in Flat

Hill. He was older; his family occupied one of the higher rungs on the short social ladder. His father owned the hardware store and the family was well off in the small-town way that during the sixties meant they had a few things other people didn't have—the first colour TV in town, a new car every three years, running water from their own well even before the town put in the water lines. They didn't show off, though. Old Paul—Paul's father—was nice to everyone. This was good for business of course, but he was the sort who would have been pleasant to people anyway.

Paul had eventually taken over the hardware business, but that was long after Mellie herself had left town. Some time in the eighties he'd allied his store with a major chain; it was the only way to keep a business like that going in a small town. The store is still there, out in Flat Hill, but he's hired someone else to run it for him. When Paul saw the chance to move to the city and buy into a flagship store in the same chain, he took it, moved to Saskatoon with Carol and the boys. Mellie's glad Paul has his finger in more than one financial pie; his first family is still in the big house in Lawson Heights and it's surprising how much money kids need for clothing and lessons and sports equipment and even for school which Mellie thought was supposed to be free.

Paul says he doesn't remember much about Mellie from back home either, says she was just a skinny kid and he'd never have recognized her if she hadn't come up to him that night at the Artful Dodger and said, "Aren't you from Flat Hill?" Mellie could do that sort of thing by then, just walk up and say that. She could do it because by then she'd found out that the divisions that kept people apart in her home town were erased by time and—mysteriously—by living in the city. And she could do it because after eighteen years at Stereo Source they'd made her assistant manager that week and she was feeling buoyant.

Once in a while, on days when Mellie is feeling particularly safe about the distance between past and present, she'll mention her mother or father, both dead for years now. Paul says he only remembers a few things about them. He remembers her mother singing *You are My Sunshine* on the stage of the town hall the night they taped the amateur hour for radio, and from that single memory he carries the inaccurate impression that she was always a cheerful woman. He remembers Mellie's dad, he says, only as the man who swept the floors at the store for a few years, never caused problems for Paul's dad, and always moved out of the way for customers.

Mellie thinks Paul remembers more than he lets on, but maybe he doesn't. Maybe history isn't terribly important to Paul. "What about the money in the jam tins?" Mellie asked him once. "You must remember the thing about the jam tins?"

"Jam tins. Jam tins?"

"There was a group of boys that used to make fun of Dad, used to say he had a fortune buried in jam tins in the backyard."

"Maybe I heard that. I don't know. I bet every town has a story like that, some character who's supposed to have a million bucks buried in the yard or under the mattress or stashed away in sacks in the root cellar."

"They believed it though," Mellie said. "They came right into the backyard once and dug holes looking for it."

"You mean they made up a story and then they believed their own story?"

There are days when Mellie feels she somehow woke up inside the wrong life. On her day off, after Paul's gone and she's loaded the breakfast dishes into the dishwasher she sits and reads the paper and drinks coffee from her favourite oversized mug. Two sugars for her sweet tooth. She feels

the house around her, the house she and Paul bought together after Paul and Carol finalized the divorce they'd been
approaching for years. Mellie likes her house so much that
sometimes she leaves the newspaper spread on the table and
walks through the rooms still carrying her coffee mug. She
stares into a Robert Hurley print or sits in the armchair and
looks at the piano Paul inherited from his grandmother.
Keys reflected in the glossy wood. Leafy shapes carved into
the front legs. She walks upstairs and makes the bed and
watches the light and the wind move through the elm
branches that shade the bedroom window. She touches the
wall lightly as she passes through the hallway, comes back
down to the kitchen and looks out the window at the six
kinds of lilies that bloom all at once in the backyard.

Earlier today, Paul picked up the kids from Carol's place
and took them out east of the city to see the damage from
the tornado. Mellie declined to go along. It isn't that she
doesn't like the boys. In fact, she enjoys the time she spends
with them. They're good boys, well-mannered for teenagers, rarely bored with themselves. More likely bound for
university than for the hardware business. In some ways it's
a shame she only sees them on the weekends. But today she
doesn't feel any need to join an expedition to see property
damage. There's enough of that on the TV news.
      This year tornadoes and other fierce winds are a regular
occurrence, it seems, and it's still only June. There is no
explanation and there are a dozen explanations. People talk
about climate change, about volcanoes erupting in the Pa-
cific and skewing the weather patterns, about the end of the
millennium or the end of the world. When Mellie was a
girl, any wind powerful enough to toss houses around and
kill people and animals was rare, wasn't it? Something that
happened in books or movies or the United States. Which
was why the one tornado she could remember had created
such excitement.

"Remember the tornado in Blake," she'd said to Paul last night.

"You mean when we were kids?"

"Yeah."

"Vaguely," he said. "I never went to see."

Mellie Sonter, twelve years old, sat leaning against the brick wall of Flat Hill school, high up on the iron fire escape platform. She'd just finished carving her initials into the soft sand-coloured brick beside the fire door, using a nail someone else had left up there, probably after doing the same thing. She sat forward and looked around. From here, she could see all the way out to the highway if she looked south; if she turned around and looked north, she could see past the grain elevators and the railway tracks and out to the water tower. She heard cars going by on the highway, dull rumbles. She heard sparrows singing in the elm trees that bordered the schoolyard and she heard the empty metal rings on the flagpole ting-tinging with the wind in the purposeless way they did all through July and August when the janitor didn't raise the flag.

Mellie loved to sit here; up here she had a kind of power. Even if someone mean or someone who made her nervous cut though the schoolyard, odds were they wouldn't see her; they'd have no reason to look up. She would call out if she saw someone she wanted to talk to—sometimes she startled people on purpose that way—or she could just keep quiet if she didn't want to be noticed.

As Mellie surveyed the schoolyard and its surroundings, Linda Murphy came out of the house across the street. She was one of the principal's daughters, a girl with bleached skin, pale eyes that were barely blue, limp hair that was a weak shade halfway between brown and grey, a girl so colourless you wanted to pick up a crayon and fill her in. Linda crossed the street to the schoolyard and lay on her stomach on the teeter-totter, slanted upward, with a book

39

in front of her.

Linda had latched on to Mellie this summer, as she had last summer. Summer was Mellie's time of year. She never felt quite at home in the ordered world of the school year, though she did all right with the work—she'd never flunked a single test. But in the summertime she could pick and choose what she did, could do whatever made her feel good. In summer, girls like Linda were more friendly toward her, girls who didn't seem to know what to do with themselves if their time wasn't organized for them by someone else. Linda came looking for Mellie sometimes in the summer. She let Mellie make decisions about where they should go, what they should do for fun. She even let Mellie boss her around a little.

"Hey Linda," Mellie shouted. "Look where I am." Linda looked up, her hand shading her eyes so Mellie could hardly see her face.

"Come on up."

Linda left her book and came puffing up the fire escape. Her steps shook the platform slightly and the soles of her runners made a dull ringing sound against the iron stairs.

"Sixteen, seventeen, eighteen," Linda said, counting the stairs the way they did. She sat down facing Mellie on the platform.

"You hear about the tornado?" Linda asked.

Mellie looked at her.

"At Blake," Linda said. "People are driving over there to see what it did. Everyone's meeting at three o'clock at the parking-lot by the train station. Anyone with extra room in their car and anyone who needs a ride."

"You going?"

"Yeah," Linda said. "Dad's taking us."

"Can I go with you?"

"Won't be room. Sorry."

"Oh."

"Well my aunt and uncle are coming with us too." Linda said.

"Oh."

Mellie caught a ride in the last car leaving the parking-lot that afternoon. All the others had pulled away when she walked up to Mr. Gunther, who was standing by his red Dodge with the driver's door already open, and asked him if he had room for her.

"Your mum and dad say you could go?" Mr. Gunther asked her.

"Yeah, they said I could go."

"Because I'm not taking anyone if their parents don't know where they are." He looked down at her. "Get in if you're getting in," he said. "Not much room left."

Mellie took a breath and climbed into the last free spot, in the back seat beside Ox Kovach. Ox was in her class at school, but he was older; he'd been held back twice. He was usually mean to Mellie if her older brother Marty wasn't within earshot, but he couldn't bother her here, not with five other people in the car besides themselves. It was half an hour south to Blake on a dusty grid road and all the windows were down to fight the heat. Mellie's hair whipped her cheeks. A few miles into the trip, the road banked around a slough. The angle of the car as it rounded the curve pressed Ox's weight toward Mellie. As the car straightened again, the motion slid his body back to where it should be and slackened the pressure of his thigh on hers, but right away again he pressed his thick leg against her thin one and kept it there. It was nothing she could call him on; the car was crowded, Ox took up a lot of space, and there were bumps and sways to contend with. She moved herself closer to the door and he used the next bump in the road as an excuse to follow.

When they finally stopped in Blake, at the edge of town where the tornado had hit, she opened the door and hardly waited for the car to stop properly before she scrambled out. Ox was close behind. He leaned down in her direction, spoke quietly so no-one else could make out the words, "Smelly Mellie, if I marry you, can we dig up all the money your old man has buried in the back yard?"

She walked away. She knew how to handle this; she was used to saying "As if I care," over and over inside her head until she just about meant it. Ox walked away in one direction and Mellie went another. People wandered in ones and twos among the torn-apart houses and trailers, people from home and people she didn't know, from other towns. The tornado had touched down right at the edge of town and a farmyard had taken part of the hit. Mellie saw a grain auger that was bent back on itself like a giant hairpin. She walked over to what used to be a house. The ragged wood smelled wet from the rain that had come with the tornado.

"Just look at this house," a woman beside her said to anyone who'd listen. She seemed almost pleased. She was a slim woman, wearing a print, A-line skirt, picking her way through the mess in a polished pair of flats, as if she were on her way to church. "Reduced to a pile of sticks," she said.

But they weren't sticks at all. They were boards and half-walls, and most of the roof was still intact, as if you could jack it up to its former height if only you had sound walls to go underneath it.

"Look at the devastation," the same woman said to a well-dressed man coming toward her through the remains of a vegetable garden. He wore pants with a crease and a pressed white shirt with a loosened tie. "The potato beetles survived the tornado," he said as if he were in some way proud of their fortitude. The woman tore a scrap of powder blue wallpaper from an exposed wall. "Just look at the devastation," she repeated.

Mellie walked across the road to the remains of a house trailer. A boy who'd been shuffling through nearby piles of

42

rubbish looked up. "That's my house," he said. He must have been about the same age as Mellie, because their eyes were at the same level when she met his look. His hair was dull brown, and parted so that a loose fan of it hung in front of one eye. He pushed his bottom lip out and blew straight up so the hair lifted for a second, then resettled.

Two men stood close to Mellie and the boy, shaking their heads over a toppled pine tree, its roots spread in the air like a many-fingered hand, looking for something to grab hold of. "I heard this is all because of the Russians and their nuclear testing," one of them said. "All the weather patterns are messed up this year and that's what it's from."

"You better believe it," said the other man.

"Look," the boy said to Mellie. He lifted a corner of aluminum and wallboard that used to be a trailer wall. He pointed underneath. "That's my room," he said.

The wind had taken the trailer apart and left it in half a dozen twisted heaps. When Mellie followed the boy's gesture and peered underneath the wall she saw a yellow, diamond-patterned floor and the corner of what might be a green curtain or bedspread. "Wow," she said. "That's something. You're sure lucky."

"I wasn't in there," he said. "I would've been, but my mum's baby came yesterday. Dad took her to the hospital last night just about an hour before the tornado hit, and I went over to my aunt's house." He pointed to a grey-and-white two-storey a few houses away that had no more damage than random patches of missing shingles and a split maple tree in the front yard.

"You shoulda heard the noise," he said. "Like ten trains all at once. My aunt made us go down to the basement and the next minute it was over and done with."

"Yeah?"

"Yeah. That's not all. Come here, I gotta show you something," he said.

Mellie hesitated. She didn't want to lose track of Mr.

Gunther, didn't want to miss her ride back. The boy had walked away without looking to see if she was with him, but he hadn't gone far. He stopped near a power pole. Mellie followed. Two men were belted near the top of the pole working with a thick black power line.

"See that wire there," the boy said. "This morning it was down here on the ground. It was live. Jumping and sparking."

"You mean live like it could electrocute someone?" Mellie said.

He nodded. "I touched it," he said. He nodded again.

"You couldn't have," she said. "You'd be dead."

"I did it."

Mellie could see people moving toward the parked cars. She wanted to get back to Mr. Gunther's car soon enough that she wouldn't end up beside Ox for the half-hour ride back to Flat Hill. She looked at the boy's face once more and said, "I gotta go. See ya."

"See ya," he said.

At the supper table that night, conversation started and ended with the tornado.

"I heard some people went over to Blake this afternoon," Mellie's father said. "To have a look at what the tornado done. Want to drive over there after supper Queenie?"

"Sure," said her mother. "Might be a nice ride. You kids should come too. Want to come?"

Marty snorted. Mellie said no thanks but didn't tell them she'd already seen it.

Their father ignored Marty's snort. "Some people say it's the Russians and their nuclear testing. Messes up the weather."

Marty snorted again, then let the snort grow into a laugh that sounded made up for the benefit of those who could hear it, rather than for his own pleasure.

"Don't laugh," Mellie's father said. "You explain it then.

44

Tornadoes don't come around too often."

"It's like that blackout a few years ago," Mellie's mother said. "Where the electricity went off all through New York and there, in the States. The TV news said it could be the Russians. They said: Just think what one Russian with a pair of pliers could do. You never know."

Marty ended up going down to Blake with their parents in spite of his pretended disinterest, but Mellie stayed home. "Fine," her mother said. "You can do the dishes then." And she did do the dishes, up to the pots and pans at least. Rather do that than go somewhere with her parents.

She didn't mind being with them as long as it was only family. Her parents left their kids alone for the most part, didn't interfere with what they did unless they got into full-scale trouble. What made Mellie shrink from being seen with her parents in public was her certainty that people could guess at every detail of their lives just by looking at them. Her mother wouldn't have embarrassed her so much if it hadn't been for her teeth. They were hard to look at, an unhealthy and uneven brown, crowded and crooked, with gaps in odd places. Mellie thought there should be a way to cover them up, at least partly, thought her mother should learn to put her hand in front of her mouth. She could have been a country and western singer if she were prettier. She could chord a song on her guitar after she'd only heard it a few times. She liked to sing *Whisperin' Pines* and the one about the wooden Indian who fell in love with an Indian maid, and she was practising *Cryin'*. She hardly strained except for the very highest notes and if you looked somewhere else, you forgot all about the teeth for the time you were listening.

Mellie's parents rarely went by their ordinary names—Charlie and Sylvia. They had special names for each other. Her father called her mother Queenie, and even Marty used that nickname for her most of the time, though he sometimes said, without appearing to care for her feelings, that it sounded like something you'd call a favourite dog.

Mellie's mother had nicknamed her husband Bing because he looked a little like Bing Crosby, she said. Mellie had seen Bing Crosby on TV and there was no resemblance. Her mother said it was from when they were all of them a lot younger. Bing wasn't the only name he went by at home. When the kids came along, Queenie had started once in a while calling her husband Pop. The two of them made a joke out of the fact that both her names for him were like imitations of sounds. Bing. Pop. Little noises.

Bing had a weak leg and trouble finding a steady job since the lumber yard let him go when business dropped off two years ago. He looked more like a farm hand than like Bing Crosby. He wore overalls almost every day. His face had a soft, disorganized look to it—cushions under his eyes and shallow, soft tucks in front of his ears and hair that wouldn't stay where it was meant to. He swept floors for the storekeepers and at Phil Gunther's garage and he drove his half-ton around town delivering groceries for Nichol's Red and White. He was good-natured for the most part but when he got mad he heated up and his face went red and then he'd explode. Hot as Hawaii when he's mad, Queenie said about Bing. His anger almost always had something to do with the mischief Marty found himself in the middle of from time to time.

Bing called Mellie his pixie girl and gave her bear hugs that squeezed the air out of her lungs. If he spent too long at the beer parlour (which didn't happen often) and came home sick and threw up he sometimes came and woke up his pixie girl to help him wipe the vomit off the floor where he'd overshot the toilet. They had to be very quiet so as not to wake Mellie's mother. Queenie didn't get mad often either, but when Bing went off alone and came home drunk she'd scream and hit. Her own father had been a drunk, she'd remind them all. A drunken old fart, she'd shout and then she'd say something about money and go upstairs and push the bedroom door shut as far as it would go before it scraped to a stop at the place where the floorboards slanted.

Mellie's brother Marty had two sides, the side she loved and the side that made her cold and scared. He was mean to her in front of other people and good to her when he thought no-one else would catch him at it. He taught her to steal chocolate bars from the Red and White store and let her keep what she smuggled out for herself. She took Oh Henrys mostly. She ate them slowly, made herself notice each bite, because they were only good for as long as they lasted and then there was a letdown.

Guys didn't mess much with Marty. He didn't go to school anymore, but he'd done Grade 9 in reform school after he'd been caught three times siphoning purple gas from farmers' tanks and selling it out of jerry cans. There'd been some business with a lawyer from Ripley, and a series of arguments between their mum and dad, with Queenie defending Marty, sometimes energetically and sometimes half-heartedly. Mellie wasn't in on the details and that was by choice. Whenever the shouting started she slipped upstairs to her room. She had a way of making a tent by draping a blanket between the iron bedstead and a wooden chair with a square frame that she could clothespin the blanket to. Sitting under the tent got to be one of her favourite pastimes and she even did it once in a while for no reason, when there was no fight to hide from. Marty was sent away for almost a year and Mellie learned to make herself think, *As if I care,* when people talked about him in front of her as if she weren't related.

Marty came home with the only real tattoo in town. He'd met up with a scratcher in reform school who'd bought a tattoo instrument through the mail. He'd drawn an American eagle—the only pattern he knew—on Marty's left arm. The lines of the picture ran from thick to thin and thick again. Parts of it weren't clear at all. Queenie gave Marty a look of disgust when she saw the tattoo. Bing said it didn't make sense for a Canadian to have a picture of an American eagle on his arm.

"You can't take that thing off you know," he said. "It'll be there till you die."

"That's right," Marty said. "That's the point."

"What's the eagle supposed to mean?"

Marty snorted. "All it's supposed to mean is that it's mine. Nobody takes it away. Who cares what the picture is? It's my arm and I can put on it what I want."

The day after she went to see the aftermath of the Blake tornado, Mellie saw Linda again at the schoolyard.

"I met a boy," she told Linda. "Over in Blake."

"Is he cute?"

"Yeah, he's cute. His trailer got smashed, but nobody was in it. Did you see it, all the walls bent just like they were made out of cardboard?"

Linda shook her head. "I hardly saw anything. Dad wouldn't let us out of the car. We drove around once and went home. What's his name?"

Mellie thought quick, thought of her cousin in Ripley, borrowed his name. "Larry," she said. Mellie knew how to lie without even thinking about it. Linda was paying attention. Mellie felt herself quicken the way she always did when people paid that kind of attention. She went on. "He said there's a sports day in Blake next Saturday and he could meet up with me if I can get there."

"Are you going?" Linda said.

"Maybe."

The *Advance* ran a feature on the Blake tornado. There was a photograph of the bent grain auger and one of the boy who'd talked to Mellie. He was helping his father lift an accordioned sheet of metal that had been part of their trailer. The man had a serious look but the boy wore an almost-grin. His hair hung down in front of one eye. The paper didn't give their names.

Off to one side a few paragraphs were boxed in under the heading, "How the Tornado Happened." The explanation made no reference to Russians or nuclear testing. *To understand a tornado you have to think of air as a massive, moving entity. A tornado results when a complicated pattern of updrafts and downdrafts cause the base of a thundercloud to rotate. In this case, a cool, moist air mass with easterly winds at ground level collided with another, warmer air mass moving southwest, five to ten thousand feet up in the air. They twirled themselves together with increasing speed and became a tornado.*

Someone came one night and dug holes in Sonters' back yard. There was no way to know who did it. It might have been Ox and his pals, it might not. Mellie heard her father shouting from the back door in the middle of the night. She heard quick footsteps beat past the house and away down the gravel street. When she went out the next morning she saw three big holes in the part of the yard they still called the garden even though no-one had planted so much as a carrot or a marigold there in years. Whoever dug the holes had used the spade and the pitchfork that usually leaned against the house underneath the kitchen window and abandoned them in the garden when they ran off. There was another spade, one they must have brought themselves, sticking up out of the dirt, its handle splintering into the air where it had broken off when the clay resisted too strongly.

The biggest hole, at the back of the garden, was almost two feet deep and as wide as an armchair. Mellie spent the next several days enlarging it, digging it deeper, making it square, straightening the sides into solid walls. The dirt below the topsoil layer was mostly clay, which was heavy to dig but behaved well when Mellie slapped the walls into shape with the broken spade or the palms of her hands. Neither her parents nor Marty asked what she was doing.

An assortment of weathered boards had leaned against

the side of the house under cover of the caraganas for as long as Mellie could remember. When she started dragging them to the garden and laying them across her hole to make a roof, her dad came out with the hammer and worked the rusty nails out, some of them at least.

"Looks good," he said. "You'll need a step down inside."

She left an opening at one end and set a shallow wooden apple box—also from the pile under the hedge—at the bottom to make climbing in and out manageable. She couldn't stand up inside, but she could sit comfortably. Inside her dirt cave she cut designs on the walls with a stick and carved cubbyholes to keep things in and built clay platforms for candles. When she was inside, the hole smelled comfortably of flame and warm wax.

Mellie never invited friends to her real house but she brought Linda Murphy over to see her hole in the garden. They hunkered down inside. The girls sat facing each other with their knees up and their backs to the dirt walls. They giggled and talked and Mellie told Linda things that weren't necessarily true. She said her mum and dad were saving up to take her on a trip to Banff to see the bears. She said she was having her periods already, had been for months. She told Linda to get the box of wooden Eddy matches out of the cubby hole in the wall and she lit a candle.

"You're allowed to have candles in here?" Linda said.

"I don't know. I just have them."

"You could start a fire you know."

"I did once," Mellie said.

"Really? You really had a *fire?*"

"Burned two of the roof boards before I could put it out. Had to find new ones."

"I don't believe you," Linda said. "How'd you put it out?"

Mellie kept her eyes on the candle she'd just lit, moved it down to a lower platform, sniffed the wooden match in her

hand to smell the spent sulphur. "Water from the rain barrel," she said.

"All by yourself?"

"Swear to god," said Mellie.

After Linda went home for supper, Mellie stayed
crouched inside her hideaway house and looked out through
the opening at the two-and-a-half slumping storeys of the
real house. If a tornado came and took it apart, they'd have
to find another place to live. That would be fine. As for her
own little underground space, Mellie made an effort to
storm-proof it. She got Marty to help her roll four old tires
across the yard and arrange them over the roof boards as
weights. He even put rocks inside some of them for extra
weight. He stopped when the job bored him. Mellie half
expected a tornado but summer slipped away with nothing
more than one dump of slushy hail in August.

It was a cold day in late November. A Saturday, a day for
chores. Dick Heise, the water man from Ripley, came by
and lowered four blocks of ice into the half-empty water
barrel in the corner of the kitchen. Other houses had running water, but Bing and Queenie were still saving up to
run the pipes into the house and do the plumbing. Mellie's
mother gave her the usual job, standing on a chair and stirring the glassy bricks of ice around in the water with a
broomstick—or trying to stir them. It was an awkward task
for someone Mellie's size but Queenie was convinced it
made the ice melt faster, and she wanted to wash clothes.

Dick Heise had brought some news with him and hadn't
been shy about telling it. "You know they're looking for
your boy?" he said to Bing.

"My boy?" Bing said.

"Marty. That's your boy, right?"

"Yes."

"Someone said he's the one tried to sell a hot socket set
over in Ripley. Phil Gunther had already phoned to the

garages in all the towns around to be on the look-out. Said he missed it first thing this morning."

Bing turned away, walked to the table, picked up his cigarette papers, opened his can of Export and rolled himself a smoke.

"The fellow in the garage would've been suspicious anyway," Dick said. "A teenager walking in with a good socket set like that. As soon as he started asking questions the boy took off in a big hurry."

Bing stood at the table and smoked. Dick took his ice money from Queenie and left. Bing opened the door of the cupboard beside the fridge. The keys for the hardware and for the Red and White and for the lumber yard were all on their nails, but the keys for Phil Gunther's garage were missing.

The back of his neck reddened and the next second he exploded. "So now Queenie. You going to stick up for him this time?"

Queenie put her purse away in the drawer, moved along the counter, swept up some crumbs with the side of her hand, put a loaf of bread away in the bread-box. She sat down. "Wait and hear what he has to say at least," she said.

Bing sat at the table with coffee and his cigarette. He watched the door as if he dared Marty to come through it. He sat for a long time. No-one said a word. Mellie kept pushing the ice around. She could see rainbows way in the middle of the ice blocks. They appeared and disappeared according to how the light fell.

There was no waiting to hear what Marty had to say for himself when he finally came home. He walked in the door with a cold rush of winter air and a false grin which he lost in the split second before Bing was on him with both fists. Mellie and her mother moved from one corner of the kitchen to the other to keep out of the way. The fight started too quickly for Mellie to run away upstairs, and once it was on she couldn't make her legs take her out of the room, couldn't stop watching the confusion of moving bodies. Arms and legs, feet and fists and elbows. Landing hard, kicking, rolling free, jumping up. Mellie felt as if two big hands were inside her, squeezing her stomach; blood pumped noisily inside her head. Marty was young and tall and well-muscled. Bing wasn't quite so tall, nor quite so big around the biceps, but he moved as if he knew what he was doing. His weak leg exaggerated the way his body rocked when he circled or moved in. Bing landed a solid punch to Marty's nose. A long, thin swirl of blood shot out and decorated a yellow cupboard door. When Queenie saw the blood she squatted in the corner and put her head between her knees. Mellie kept watching, heard their breath grating in and out, smelled their sharp sweat.

Bing lost the early advantage that the element of surprise had given him. The blow to the nose made Marty switch from ducking and defending to pouncing and thumping. Mellie was betting on Marty and she wasn't sure how she felt about this. Either of them might have gotten the best of the other eventually if the mounties hadn't come looking for Marty about the stolen socket set. They must have heard the commotion when they came to the door because they walked right in without knocking. The two officers were larger than life moving across the kitchen. Brown parkas, bright yellow stripes down the sides of their pants, winter hats with fur flaps tied in place across the top, the smell of winter on their clothes. One cop was beefy and the other was skinny like a mosquito with a pointed nose. The skinny cop grabbed an unresisting Bing by the shoulders and stood between him and his son while the bigger one manœuvred Marty's hands behind his back. "Marty Sonter?" he said.

The rest of that winter whenever people made remarks about her brother, Mellie was tempted to say he was reading a lot of books in jail and she bet he'd be a lawyer by the time he got out. She didn't say it though, because there are some things no-one will believe.

53

Marty does all right now. He got his Class A papers and he drives trucks all over Canada and the US. He's seen a lot of the continent from the cab of a Kenworth. He sends Christmas cards and writes short messages inside that almost make Mellie hear his voice: *Take 'er easy. Watch out for falling rocks and other shit.* He called one Saturday last fall on his mobile phone. He was at the outskirts and Mellie gave him directions for how to find the house. When Paul came in after his golf game and saw Mellie and Marty at the kitchen table, each with a drink and the rye bottle between them, he was as friendly to Marty as he'd be to anyone. "What you up to these days?" he'd said and poured a rye for himself instead of his usual scotch.

"Same old bullshit," Marty said. He didn't stay for more than the one drink but he was congenial, even warm. The lower third of the eagle tattoo, all that was visible below his T-shirt sleeve, looked unsurprising, unexceptional. He told Paul and Mellie they had a very nice place; he didn't smoke inside the house and he asked Paul how his boys were doing.

Mellie tells herself she shouldn't be surprised. She's changed too. She no longer carries herself through life on a raft of little lies the way she did when she was a girl, though she still catches herself dressing up the truth a little sometimes. After all, most of what can be said without lying is next door to boring. Even when life is good. Especially when life is good.

Mellie takes a ginger ale out of the fridge, holds the cold can against her cheek and lets a thin vein of condensation trickle down her neck. Paul won't be home for at least another hour, maybe longer depending on how captivated the boys are by the wind damage. She turns on the TV, slumps down on the couch, takes a drink of her ginger ale and feels the bubbles break as they pass down her throat. She shifts on the couch and the leather pulls at her skin where her legs are bare below her shorts.

The TV news says two teenagers from the southern US have been found guilty of manslaughter. They swiped a small-town stop sign and the next morning an accident at that intersection killed two people. It's startling how little a person can get away with. Out behind Pavelik's grain bins a few miles south of Flat Hill, where Mellie used to go to parties when she was in high school, a path led into the bush and stopped in front of a checkerboard dead-end sign nailed to a poplar tree. This was where the guys went to pee. (The girls went to a different spot, up behind the caragana bushes in what was left of the farmyard, close to the fallen-in basement.) Marty and one of his buddies had put the checkerboard sign up. Mellie wasn't sure which road they'd taken it from but she never heard of any accidents as a result of it being gone.

There's more tragedy on the news: another tornado—this one in the south of the province—and a funnel cloud sighting in Manitoba but no report that it's touched down yet. What seemed like the event of a lifetime when she was a child has somehow multiplied itself. Are there more distressing disasters out there these days, more failures of luck than there used to be? More things that could do a person damage any minute, any day? Flesh-eating diseases and accidents and crazy people with bombs.

It's a discussion she's tried to have with Paul. He says what most people say—that disasters are nothing new, it's just that the newspapers and the TV people are better at making sure we know about every little thing that goes wrong anywhere. It's a trap to worry about every remote possibility, he says. But then, Paul isn't a worrier. He isn't a worrier and he wouldn't know how much trouble some people have just believing life will hold itself together. How they always have one ear listening for the wind to suck the roof up—tires, rocks, boards and all.

.

GABRIELLA GOLIGER

In This Corner

Macho Man Randy Savage stomps down the aisle toward the ring, teeth bared, fists raised, mugging for the camera and hurling threats that are drowned out by the roaring crowd.

"More than 90,000 fans," bawls the announcer. "Madison Square Gardens is packed." His voice is already hoarse and strained with excitement. Crank it up another notch and he'll lose it, Rachel thinks. He'll screech. He'll sound like the kind of candy ass that Savage is vowing to bust into dust.

Her father sits perched on the couch in the shadows, bony legs crossed at the knees, chin in hand, a pose of mild contemplation. Rachel lingers by the basement entrance trying to make out the grey blur of his face in the flickering light. Thinner than he was the last time she saw him. Something to get used to with each visit home, this whittling away of age. Upstairs, pots and dishes clatter as her mother takes care of the aftermath of lunch. Saturday's "Raw Cuts" has become a ritual, the one sacred hour of the week. Eye on the clock as 1 PM approaches, he hurries to clean his plate and to shuffle downstairs, slippers flapping, into the gloomy darkness of the rec-room.

"Go! Go to your fat men," Rachel's mother yells after him, but he pays no attention.

He waves the wand, steps back a pace at the blast of sound, then settles himself into his corner of the couch as wrestlemania erupts on the screen.

Could be studying Michelangelo's David the way he ponders, so sober and reflective. Or perhaps it's just that old absence of his. Using the noise and clamour on the set to mask his retreat into a distant and private place that she can only guess at.

Macho Man leaps over the ring ropes and struts from

58

corner to corner in his red bodysuit, black cape and jewel-studded cowboy hat which throws out spears of light. He howls. He rips off the brim of his hat with his teeth and tosses the pieces to the outstretched hands of adoring fans. Organ music swells as the opponent, Yokozuna, the Sumo wrestler, lumbers into view, a vat of a man, massive belly jiggling over his belt. The upward slant of his eyes is accentuated with black lines. His hair is tied into a top knot. Ninety thousand boos rock the hall.

The men begin the careful, choreographed performance. They grunt, butt, sail into the air, thud down on the mat. They twist each other into impossible knots and pound the floor with feet and fists.

Rachel tries to fathom her father's expression.

"How can you watch this stuff?" she asks yet again.

"They're usually well-matched," he says, slow and considering. "But I'm not so sure about today. It may not be a fair fight."

"But Dad, you can't still believe it's real."

Ernst Birnbaum, 81 years old, spare and withered, five-foot-five in his down-at-heel slippers, 125 pounds and losing, slowly. Flesh dripping away with the years. But the sober dignity in his features remains. The Old World cultivation. A breeze of sidewalk cafés, onionskin newspapers, civilized pessimism wafts about his shoulders. All his life, the skeptic, the realist. Embarrassed by displays of woolly sentiment. Even the singing of the national anthem in movie theatres used to make him twitch. A dry "we'll see," was all he had to say to Trudeaumania. And yet he was always so easily wounded by the wounds of the smallest creatures. Rachel recalls the severed worm he found on one of their walks when she was a child. It returns in her dreams, raw and bloody, rising, quivering, falling to the sidewalk. He dropped her hand and lifted the thing between his forefinger and thumb to place it on the grass. She thrust her treasonous fists into her pockets, unable to grasp again his worm-slimed hand.

And now this. Macho madness, the roars and bellows, the sweat and spit.

A commercial break interrupts the action and Brutus Beefcake presses his face up close to tell fans about an upcoming match.

"I'm gonna squash his brains. You're toast buddy, you're a Timbit, I'm gonna eat you for breakfast...."

"The whole thing is staged, Dad. It's so obvious."

He shakes his head and smiles almost sadly, as if she is the one who is under illusions.

He still takes the train to the office in the mornings, but, once there, holds his head in his hands, watches from his backroom desk as Rachel's brother Avi cuts the deals. He is tired. He has earned his tiredness, Rachel thinks. And his doubts. When Avi swings into the back room to tell him the latest—all their Sunseeker tours to the Caribbean booked, extra flights on order—his face wavers between pleasure and caution. For decades he toiled away in the dusty one-room travel agency, transformed it finally, before Avi took over, into a plate-glass storefront on a minor downtown artery.

All his life hedging his bets, methodical and prudent, searching for some flat, narrow ground between extremes.

Macho Man moonsaults from the top of the ropes, but misses his opponent and seems to land on his head, which he holds and shakes as he stumbles to his feet.

"How can it be fake when you see what they do to one another?" her father asks, eyes still on the set.

"If it's real, how can you stand it?"

"But they're trained for it. And usually it's an even match." A grave nod. A dry little cough.

Rachel's mother thumps down the stairs and into the gloom of the basement. She wipes her dishwater-wet hands in her apron, glances at the screen, snorts with disgust.

"Pfui, those fat men, like slabs of beef."

"You're talking to the wall." Rachel moves over to where her mother is standing. She catches Hannah's eye and instantly they both hoot with laughter. They are weak with hilarity. Her mother's strained face becomes soft and warm, like a blanket shaken out in the sun.

"How they smack themselves around." Hannah wipes tears from her eyes.

"If you don't watch out he'll turn up the volume."

"Why can't he watch a good film with me?" Hannah's tone changes. "Last night Greta Garbo was on and he leaves in the middle to go to bed."

Just as always, ever since Rachel can remember. Her parents were on the couch, Hannah at one end, Ernst at the other, washed in the glow of vintage black-and-white. Her mother sat engrossed. It was what Hannah wanted—a decent love story that dug deeply into the human heart. Her father sat stiff and dutiful on his side for as long as he could stand it, then rose abruptly, pecked them both on the cheek and was gone.

And yet Hannah's complaints have lost their edge. They have a resigned ring to them. The triumph of ridicule. The comfort of long-established routine, of knowing where to find him. In the old days, when Rachel had still lived at home, the air snapped with bitterness, desire stifled.

It would start with a thread.

He sat in his armchair in the living-room, stone-still, head slightly raised and eyes looking downwards through bifocals at the book held in front of him. Churchill's *History of World War II*. He was plodding his way through all six volumes, beginning with *The Gathering Storm* and ending with *Triumph and Tragedy*. Her mother, finished with the lunchtime dishes, crept down the hall to see if he was asleep and finding him awake, stood uncertain in the doorway. She watched for a moment, then plopped down in a chair opposite, heaving a sigh. Rachel lying on the couch allowed her own book to fall from her hands and met her mother's eyes, pulled despite herself toward Hannah's need. Her mother's hands flew palm-up in the air in a gesture of bewilderment, impatience, despair. *What do you want? Leave us alone*, Rachel said silently. She could not speak out loud, knowing how easy it was to tilt the equilibrium of the room, set off a string of explosions. Her father turned a page.

"Ernst, do you want a cup of tea?" Hannah's question sounded like a threat.

"Not now." His voice muffled and distant, as if coming from the bottom of a well.

"I want to show you my new dress now, all right? I need to know what you think."

A noise from his side of the room like a grunt, or a clearing of the throat.

She marched down the hall. Rachel could not help but listen for the squeak of drawers, the rustle of paper, the rattle of the mirror on the closet door. Eager, desperate sounds.

"Well, what do you think?"

She stood before him in the purple dress, hands fluttering, shoulders stiff, one higher than the other. It was always the same dress. A simple shirtwaist of cheap, shiny material bought at Ogilvy's bargain basement. Hannah's stomach pressed against the belt that accentuated her thickened waistline. He had given up trying to get her to spend money on more flattering clothes. Always he met with unfathomable resistance.

"It's fine." His eyes flicked up and then down again.

"Look at me, for godsakes."

Churchill fell with a thud onto her father's knees.

"There's a thread hanging."

"Where, where?" She whipped around.

"There! There!" He bent down and jerked at the long wisp of purple that hung from her hem.

"You don't like it, do you? And now I can't give it back. But look at the colour. Look how nice."

His words came in an angry hiss that made Rachel shiver.

"It's the kind of dress that the women who cleaned toilets back home would wear."

Yokozuna lifts Macho Man above his head, shuffles around the ring with him as if he were a trophy and hurls him to the floor.

"Sheeyah, look at that," her father says, hugging himself.

Macho Man retaliates with a knuckle thrust to his opponent's eye, toppling him backwards like a bowling pin. The Man grins, making hand-wiping gestures to the audience, while behind his back the Sumo wrestler climbs the ropes. The audience shrieks and groans, but it's no use. The brute drops ass-first onto his prey.

"Ach, poor guy. But what can you expect? An unfair match."

"Pfuiyah! Makes me want to vomit!"

"It's not real, Mum. It's all a show."

"What difference does it make? Come with me outside."

But Rachel lingers. She leans against the armrest of the couch letting the din of Madison Square Gardens wash over her while Hannah clumps back up the stairs.

Yokozuna lifts Macho Man by his hair and the seat of his pants and thunks him headfirst against the ring-post. Ninety thousand fans moan in protest, but Ernst is silent. She wonders if his interest is feigned after all. He refolds his arms across his chest, presses his cold, old-man hands into his armpits and continues to watch, or to dream, or to doze. It is easier for her to imagine the young man she never knew, the mist of possibilities he presents, than the father who sits beside her with his long, long life wound up

63

tightly inside him.

He had told her so often about his home town, sometimes with nostalgia, sometimes with bitterness. He knew every back alley and every path in the adjacent woods. It was a famous spa town of western Bohemia. Villas and cafés, hotels and promenades piled up in the valley that was tucked between steep, green hills. The centrepiece of the town was a hotspring that shot up 40 feet before collapsing upon itself, seeming to strain toward the ceiling of the glass hall that had been built around it. Visitors from all over Europe and America came to sip its salty, medicinal waters.

She had learned early on that the Europe of the time when he was young had been like an elegant banquet table, covered with starched linen, laden with gleaming china and silver platters, but with a large hidden hole cut in the middle. An evil gnome sat beneath, tugging the cloth downwards. Anyone with his eyes open, he said, could see that a crash was on its way.

His moment of decision came on a fine June day while he stood on a curb sniffing the pine-scented air. A procession of about 50 brown-shirted men rounded the corner at the bottom of the street and marched toward him.

She imagines how it was. They sing as they approach, arms swinging, mouths falling open and shut. A song about verdant hills and the erasing of unnatural borders. Her father regards their exalted, reddened faces, the suffocating intensity in their eyes. A few townspeople turn away, many others wave. Among the marchers he recognizes an optometrist, a former school chum, several teachers from the high school, the owner of the hair salon on Schillerplatz. They move forward, unselfconscious, as if pulled by a string. A young girl passes out flyers proclaiming a rally of the Sudeten German Party. He wants to hurl himself against the line of forward marching bodies, smash at least one of those upward tilted chins against the curb. He wants to roar out a string of obscenities. Instead, he presses his lips together. He pulls himself up into a straight-backed, rigid stance, eyes fixed on the gilded clock-face across the street.

Soon afterwards, he was gone, marching toward the border with a small knapsack on his back. In the grey stillness of the morning, on the empty country road, he must have felt carefree as a child. Free of that pretty, narrow-minded town, alone in the immense, godless silence. He had everything he wanted—a landscape large enough to disappear in.

But a few months later, loneliness pressed in as he lay on his cot in the kibbutz, surrounded by the yip and yowl of jackals. One evening he bowed to a young woman in a dance hall, a gesture so formal and eager, she burst into brilliant laughter. He was charmed by the reckless way she kicked up her heels while dancing the *hora*, her sudden red-faced awkwardness when a dress button came undone, how she fumbled with large, trembling fingers. He wanted to protect, guide, enfold her.

When did his disenchantment begin? When did her need of him become a burden? Did he one day lean toward her intending a brief hug and find her arms locked around him? Did he pry her off as one might a child who makes a drama of going to bed in the dark?

Rachel would come home to the bedroom door shut tight, a terrible silence behind it. Her father would be in his place in the living-room, glued to the spot, facing Churchill. There was nothing to be said. Rachel would steel herself and enter the bedroom where Hannah lay hunched up, face to the wall, as clay-heavy as the drowned. It was up to Rachel to effect the slow resuscitation. She touched Hannah's tear-stained face, stroked her hair, reasoned, encouraged, begged. Rachel's hands shook with tenderness and loathing, with the need to pull her mother up from the deep and the temptation to push her under. And where was he? High and dry on his island of indifference. If she could yank him from his chair, hurl him to his knees by the bed. If she could look him in the eye with her accusations. But he had never turned on Rachel with that cold, annihilating stare that made her mother flail and scream. And she was not about to put him to the test.

The referee, absurd in his white shirt and bow tie, dances about, jabbing a finger in the air. Both men are on the floor, Yokozuna leaning over Macho Man with one great arm wrapped around his opponent's neck. They lie still for some moments and it would seem that they've decided to take time out, but then a microphone picks up the whistle of breath and a sound like strangled retching.

Ernst looks up at her and smiles. He pats the couch beside him.

"Sit down dear," he says and so she does, leaning her shoulder against him. He tucks her arm under his, the old, familiar gesture of their Sunday walks together.

It was always possible to achieve a truce. Sensing the moment, Rachel would take her mother's hand and lead her to where he sat. By then he would be uneasy and abashed, arms pressed against his chest.

"Well then, shall we put this behind us," he would say with a cough, as his eyes slid sideways. Not the tender reconciliation Hannah wanted but a reprieve of sorts.

"I'm not the one who quarrelled." Her lame effort to squeeze something more out of the occasion.

He would dart a kiss to the side of Hannah's head, her arms would encircle him. Her tear-swollen face pressed against his neck while he stood stiff, hands dangling. His eyes when they met Rachel's would have a muddy, helpless look.

66

The crowd erupts. Waves of chanting. Ninety thousand voices knitted together. Both men are down again, writhing on the canvas. Yokozuna clasps his knee, Savage hugs his chest, while the referee cavorts around them, swinging his arm up and down as if clanging an invisible bell. Then, on cue it seems, both men begin to stagger upward, shaking their massive heads.

Sweat-drenched, reeling like drunkards they collide once more and collapse onto the canvas.

"This is incredible, folks. The punishment these guys are taking. And they're getting up. I can't believe this. They won't give up."

It is this, Rachel realizes, that her father is waiting for, what holds him here in this darkened, musty basement on a sunny afternoon. The sight of two punch-drunk hulks, blind with exhaustion and wrenched with pain, staggering to their feet. He leans forward, and excitement flickers across his face. He grunts softly as his mind pushes upward, heaves against gravity along with Macho Man. His hands grope in the air, they miss, and he must dodge, stumbling backwards, in danger of being crushed one final, fatal time. He whirls around with a sudden burst of energy, hooks his arm under Yokozuna's armpit and does the impossible, heaves the massive body up, up and onto his shoulder, where it teeters, a mountain suspended in space. Then over and down to crashing defeat. Palms upraised in a victor's stance, he greets the thunderous applause.

"Ha, ha," her father says. His voice flies up an octave. "You see! You see!"

Calling

All that is still recognizable of Ernst Birnbaum is his ear. It is erect and robust, gilded with the remnants of a Florida tan, standing at attention on his shrunken head. It is turned toward Rachel as she gazes down at her father in the hospital bed. She'd know that ear anywhere. The rest of him is a wasted fetal form, a limp, grey-skinned fledgling on a pavement. Unbelievable this process, how each day he dissolves more, each day is less distinguishable from the grey-green hospital gown, veteran of a thousand thousand launderings.

Rachel touches the rim of her father's ear with her fingertips. Cold. But ears usually are. She brings her mouth close. Supposedly hearing is the last sense to go.

"Dad, it's me Rachel. Your Rachele. Dad, I'm here. I love you Dad."

Useless words. As useless as the colourless fluid that a few days ago still dripped from a plastic pouch above his head through a tube into his veins and through another tube out again. I'm here, I love you, I'm Rachel. Repeated and redundant, swallowed up in the cavern. Cold breath on congealing waters.

Days ago, when he was still responding. Lifetimes ago, when she was still able to rush around and find small ways to bring comfort. While her mother stroked his face with trembling fingers or stood stricken in the corridor outside his room, Rachel dashed through streets and shopping malls returning quickly, quickly, with helpful things—a duck-down quilt from home, a portable radio/tape player with earphones, giant-sized Kleenexes, a large-faced wall clock. She manoeuvred the car through city traffic to fret at the interminable, ungodly tie-ups in the hospital parking-lot. Incredible. A man can have wasted away to a skeleton, his heart knocks against his ribs with a cold that thin hospital blankets do nothing to mitigate, yet the lot attendant yawns. The ticket machine sticks out a blue tongue. The swing arm creaks up, lets a car inch forward, creaks down.

She tucked the quilt around him. She fed him Strauss waltzes through the earphones of the portable player. She stuck the wall clock to the wall because he could no longer see the thread-thin hands of his wristwatch and because a nurse suggested it would help ground him to know the time of day.

"Are you all right dear?"

Nurse Judy Kimber, blond and rosy and uniformed in pink, slips into the room, then with a pat to Rachel's shoulder, out again. A good ten years younger than Rachel and calling her "dear" but with no disrespect intended. Rachel has heard Judy call her father "sweetie" and "darling" as she cradled his head in her hand, feeding him broth. This is the oncology ward, such excesses are normal, Judy is a candy-coloured angel.

The second-hand jerks forward around the circle. Four-thirty-four and twenty-eight seconds. Pain has subsided. Silence bears down on the dim-lit room. Nevertheless his ear beckons, open, receptive, a cup into which she could pour, what? Confessions, secrets, a final revelation, a magical promise? If only she had one.

His own revelation flew at her one day. It beat her face with black wings, then disappeared, dissolved into an ordinary, blue September sky.

They sat on a park bench together overlooking Lake Ontario that winked and danced in the sun. How did he get to be so old, so collapsed into himself, she wondered. Retirement was to blame. He shouldn't have stopped going to the office even at 80, even if it was just to put in time. Now he rose late in the morning, shined his shoes as always, but left them on a sheet of newspaper by the back door while he shuffled about the house in a fog of apathy.

She and her brother Avi were scheming, though, about the retirement village in Florida. Heaven's Half Acre. She had the brochure in her pocket. A gated community of white-washed condominiums surrounding an artificial lake and groomed lawns.

He leaned against her slightly on the bench, flicked peanut crumbs from his pocket at approaching sparrows.

"Great day," she ventured.

"Ach ya, beautiful." He shook his head and sighed at this beauty, amazed or bewildered by it, or perhaps doubting it would last.

"What would you like to do next, Dad? Is there something you've always dreamt of doing, but didn't get around to?"

Sparrows fluttered in the dirt at their feet. Waves lapped the shore. The smokestacks of Hamilton Harbour barely smudged the air.

"I should have gone to Auschwitz," he said in a slow, flat voice as if commenting on the probability of rain. "I had the chance a few years ago when I was in Europe, but I didn't have the nerve."

She had never heard him pronounce the name before. The profanity. Uttered in her father's cultured German. She could think of nothing to say and stared instead at an object far out on the lake, perplexed as to whether it was a buoy or a duck.

"When were you in Europe?" she said at last. She could not recall him going anywhere for years, other than to trundle back and forth to Toronto on the GO train.

"We were in Switzerland, don't you remember? Our walking holiday in Arosa? Your Aunt Hilda came to join us for the last week and I said I had to get back early because of business. I had it all planned. They stayed behind at the pension and I took the train to Zurich airport. I had the visa for Poland, I was on my way. But I couldn't go through with it." He shook his head, picked at a thread on his buttonhole with thin, dry fingers.

"But what would be the point...."

"Actually, what happened was, I got a migraine like I haven't had for years."

She could understand why he'd try to slip away without her mother knowing. A tour of ovens and gas chambers? Hannah wouldn't have allowed it. All that money, pristine mountain air, exercise and good food blown away.

"I should have done more to save my family. I know it makes no sense," he said, turning a bitter smile upon her. "But it goes through my head. That perhaps I could have done something. I think of it every day."

What family, she almost wanted to say. It had been so long since they'd been mentioned.

"But what could you have done?"

"I know."

The moment stretched out between them. She searched the lake for the buoy or the duck. A black dot that dipped and disappeared and reappeared. She took a deep breath.

"You're not getting out enough, Dad. You're too isolated and the winter will be worse. A month from now, you won't even be coming to this park."

She pulled out the brochure and explained how easy it would be, how little it would cost. Forty dollars a day for the two of them, including car rental. She pointed out the nature sanctuary nearby and read the description. "A bio-logic wonderland where visitors are rewarded by sights of alligators, rare plants, unusual animals, odd and beautiful birds."

He stared down at the picture of a wood stork, with its white-feathered body, naked head and hooked bill.

"Ach ya," he sighed. "It's an idea. I have to think about it." His voice trailed off. He plunged his hands between his crossed legs rubbing and warming them. Turned suddenly as if inspiration had struck.

"You look pale. Are you getting enough fresh air?"

71

He lifted her chin toward him in the old way, brow knitted with concern.

"I'm fine Dad. Healthy as a horse. Anyway, I'm doing aerobics twice a week."

They rose to stroll arm in arm along the seawall, his step still light and firm although he wheezed and snuffled, dabbed every few moments with his handkerchief at the perpetual drip at the end of his nose.

"Nonsense," her mother said later when Rachel told her about the conversation in the park. "He doesn't dwell on the past. He's a sensible man. We all lost family. It was a long time ago."

Family had always been the four of them—Dad, Mum, Avi and herself—self-contained, unbreakable as an atom despite the small daily explosions. There were a few relatives in faraway places—Europe, Israel—whose pale blue airletters occasionally arrived in the mailbox. There were dead relatives. She knew that. But they were nameless, once-upon-a-time people. A familiar, almost comfortable absence. The substance of shadows on a cloudy day.

Once when she was quite young she heard her father utter the words "my brothers."

Rachel was at an age when curiosity was an itch. She sensed mysteries all around her, treasures in the hidden spaces between the couch cushions. Her hands crept into drawers. Her finger poked through the torn vinyl of the kitchen chair, into the depths of its stuffing. She pricked up her ears when her parents talked in low voices, half in English, half in German. An endless drone of meaningless grown-up talk, yet sometimes magic happened. And there it was. Two words leapt hard and bright out of the fog. "My brothers."

"What brothers?"

Silence in the kitchen. Her parents shifted in their chairs. Their eyes closed down.

"Tell me. Tell me."

Her mother jumped up to the fridge, got out the chocolate pudding and scooped a shivering piece into a glass dish. Cool and slippery on the tongue.

In bed at night, though, the words came back to her.

"My brothers."

What did he mean? She had a brother, Avi. Her friends had brothers. But that was different. Her father was a grown-up. And different from any other grown-ups she knew because when he was not with them—her mother, Avi or herself—he was alone. In his chair with the newspaper or a fat book. On the balcony, staring out across the roofs of neighbouring houses. Such a man did not have brothers.

The itch got her into trouble

She had climbed out of bed to get a glass of milk. Walked into the living-room where her father sat alone on the couch—a blur in the grey wash of TV light. From down the hall came the splash of water. Her mother having a long soak in the tub.

"What are you doing here?" He squinted at her through the flickering glow.

"I'm thirsty."

"Well, hurry up."

When she came back he was leaning forward, hugging himself with his hands in his armpits. On the screen she saw a puppet in striped pyjamas reeling from side to side, but she could not see the strings that held it up. She rested her shoulder against the living-room archway and lifted her glass to her lips.

"Get out!"

She had never heard his voice like that, a sharp-toothed edge to it. He was on his feet, waving his arms and still she couldn't see his face in the gloom. She froze for a moment, then for some reason dodged around him, deeper into the

73

living-room, still clutching her glass, trapped by this beast that was not her father.

"Didn't I tell you to get out!"

She stepped backwards, almost bumped into the TV behind her and turned around as if a hand had turned her. It was not a puppet, it was a skeleton man and it was running forward with its arms raised.

A hand smacked across her thighs. Milk flew from the glass onto the carpet. As she ran from the room, the injustice crashed down on her. She had done nothing, just lingered in the doorway. The milk on the carpet was his fault. She stood in the kitchen, heart jumping, waiting for him to come after her. But he didn't.

A few minutes later she heard tinkling voices—her favourite commercial. "E - N - O, when you're feeling low, ENO!" And then he called out over the singing voices, "You can come in now." He patted the couch beside himself, tousled her hair when she sat down. They watched in silence through several more commercials—Rothman's, Pepsodent, Brylcream. When the news came on he tapped his watch.

"Off to bed," he said in his mock horrified voice.

At some point, she can't remember when, she knew about the brothers. That they stayed behind in Europe and perished in the war, while he managed to get out before it was too late. She knew their names—Thomas and Martin—although who was the older, who the younger, she'd never been able to get straight. They were both much older than her father, born in eighteen-something while he—he liked to point out—was a child of the twentieth century.

During one of their Sunday-morning walks, he told her what happened, although she remembers it more as the story of his escape than of their demise.

Rachel and her father brisk-marched up the long hill of Victoria Avenue into Westmount where the streets became

74

lazy loops, and where the trees had room to stretch out. Their destination was Summit Circle and Westmount Lookout, high above the city.

She remembers how he looked in those days. Neat, dignified, handsome with his thick, trained-back hair, beige trenchcoat, leather gloves, and of course, perfectly polished shoes.

At the beginning of Belvedere Crescent, he stopped to sniff the air. It was late October. The wind, cool on her cheeks, smelled of crushed leaves, woodsmoke and frost.

"The air in my town was fresh like this. Always. Even in summer you had the freshness from the mountains all around," he said.

He'd often told her about the town in Bohemia with its green hills and red-roofed houses strung out along the river. She knew about the family shop on the main street. They sold shoes, beautifully made shoes from Prague and Italy. He helped out in the store but, as the youngest, was the least involved in keeping the business afloat. After a few years of drifting about, he decided to get out of Europe altogether.

"My brothers thought Hitler wouldn't last, or the Allies would step in sooner. All those things that millions of others thought."

He gazed down at his feet as he walked as if searching for a flaw in the shining leather.

"But anyway, you escaped," she said, reminding him of the point of the story.

"Yes, I was lucky. While my brothers perished," his voice flat and final.

Why did people say "perished" or "lost in the war." Never died, or killed. If you were lost, you could be found again. Is that what he meant?

I think of them every day.

"Nonsense. He was never the moody type. Besides, his brothers were so much older. Grown-ups already when he was still a boy. They weren't close."

"We all lost family."

"I had an uncle," Hannah told Rachel one day. They were sitting in her parents' sun porch overlooking the back lawn, bright with sunshine.

"Uncle Morris. A kind man and a bon vivant. Not so strict religious as my father. He went to his favourite local every Saturday for herring and beer. He was big and fat and loose, but always dressed just so in a three-piece suit with a gold watch-chain dangling from his waistcoat pocket and a carnation in his lapel. My Aunt Ida put a fresh one there every morning. Uncle Morris loved fine clothes, good food and especially his schnapps. He was fat, but light on his feet. The way he sailed across the dining-room, unstoppered the crystal decanter, poured himself a glass and brought it to his nose. Such a performer. And then the way he smacked his lips and let out a big, wet *ah.*

"We children would follow him around and imitate him. Partly laughing at him, yes, such monkeys. But partly just loving the sound he made. That *ah!* He put his guts into it and it sent a thrill down your spine like a note in an aria. We wanted to do it too, but of course we couldn't. We sounded like sick cats, strutting about, patting our stomachs.

"Anyway, poor Morris went insane right after he arrived in Auschwitz." She lowered her voice, spoke in a rush, although there was no-one else around.

"I heard about it from a second cousin I met on the streets of Tel Aviv after the war. He saw them beat his Ida with whips. Who knows what for, she was half dead already when they got there. A day later, I think, he tore off his prison uniform—cap, shirt, pants, the works—and ran

76

naked to the latrine, the stinking, overflowing latrine and rolled around...."

She stopped to take a breath. Her chest heaved under her apron.

"Anyway, the point is, that's not what I think about. I think of Morris in his dining-room, with his thick fingers holding the schnapps glass like it was a flower."

"Come," she said, rising abruptly. "Come see my hedge roses."

Rachel followed her mother, who walked with arthritis-stiff and determined steps to the trellis by the back fence. Most of the blossoms were past their prime, brown at the edges, but some were still unblemished. Bursts of creamy white against the green. She raised a flower, not to her nose, but to her mouth, and turned her head from side to side to let the cool petals stroke her lips.

Thomas and Martin. She speaks their names. Speaks them out loud with the German accent that her father would use. And sees nothing. Feels nothing.

The second-hand jerks and arrives back where it was a minute ago. It is neither dark nor light, day nor night. Her father still breathes, but without movement. She has risen and fallen so long now on the tiny sea of his chest, she has lost all sense of motion.

"Take a break dear."

Judy, the pink-clad nurse, glides noiselessly to the bed, checks a plastic bag of fluid hanging down from the edge. A perfunctory check. Her job is nearly done.

Rachel gropes toward the hallway. It's long after visiting hours, yet the hall seems crowded and humming. Colours jump out at her. The lemon yellow of the walls. The metallic gleam of instruments on a trolley.

One of the patients, an old man in a plaid robe, shuffles out of his room pushing the IV tower before him. She has seen him often. He has a kicked-in looking face, wrinkle-scored and bruised, and bird's nest eyebrows. A few weeks ago he would have seemed pathetic with his trembling shoulders and painful progress. Now he seems a miracle. He can stand. He can walk. One slippered foot in front of the other, he will make it all the way down to the lounge. She moves with him. Feels the polished floor under his feet, the rush of air, hot-stabbing in his lungs. His green plaid slippers match his robe. Someone—perhaps he himself—still cares about appearances.

How long since her father last wore shoes?

He fell in a downward spiral from slippers to socks stretched over edema-swollen feet to nothing at all.

He always took special care of shoes. The Birnbaum and Sons slogan was "Shoes to last a lifetime." Once he could afford it, he bought quality—rich, soft leather, solidly stitched. He polished weekly. Sunday mornings, before breakfast, he stood in the doorway of the back fire-escape, the family's footwear lined up on newspaper in a neat row down the hall. He slipped a shoe over his left hand, examined the week's damage and began the reparations. With an old sock on his right hand, he daubed polish over the surface of the leather, rubbed firmly into every seam and crack, let the shoe stand to dry, then buffed with a brush. The hallway smelled of Cat's Paw polish and damp air from the courtyard beneath the fire-escape.

He scolded her when he caught her cramming her feet into her shoes without untying the laces.

"Show some respect for what was once alive. That is the skin of an animal."

In the armchair near her father's bed, she dreams she is wrapped in a plaid robe with an IV tube protruding from her navel. She takes the tube between thumb and forefinger and aims it at a blank television screen across the room. She points and squeezes, squeezes and points but nothing happens.

Waking, she remembers the picture of a mountain of shoes. It's in a book she's been reading off and on for the past month. She keeps it buried in the bottom of her suitcase and sneaks it out when she hears her mother settle down in the room next door. Men's, women's, children's. Boots, sandals, loafers, ordinary walking shoes. Thrown pell-mell into the heap, not a pair to seen, all singles. Mashed down, crushed, battered, all turned over time into a dull, uniform mud colour. A museum exhibit. "Confiscated from the prisoners in Majdanek," reads the caption.

How long since she last saw her father's feet? His body is a faint "S" beneath the blanket. Nestled together, his limbs take up little space. Breath seeps in and out again, washes over beached lungs. The ear seems to detach itself and hover.

Let me go in your place, she screams out in her head. She fills the air with her silent screaming.

I'll go there for you. I'll bear witness. Let me, she implores.

Surely he must hear.

Premonitions

Throughout her long life Hannah Birnbaum has remembered in detail a hiking trip she took by herself through the Giant Mountains near her home town of Breslau shortly before she left Germany for good. It was September 1933 and Hannah was eighteen. A lot was happening in Germany at the time—Hitler had come to power at the beginning of the year, there'd been the boycott of Jewish businesses, the burning of the books. Everyone in her youth group was talking emigration. But it was mainly because of Edith that the walk through the mountains etched itself into Hannah's memory. Just as Hannah was about to reach the summit of *Schneekoppe*, the highest peak on the German side of the border, she had a premonition. Her younger sister Edith was in danger. It happened in an instant, the sense of dread, unaccountable, yet as sharp as the taste of blood on the tongue. She was not a believer in such things —voices, visions—nevertheless after some hesitation she turned in her tracks and commenced the long trudge downwards through the pine-skirted slopes, her legs sore and heavy, all the joy of exploration gone out of them.

For once, Hannah had no trouble deflecting her father's questions about where she was going. She lifted her eyes to the lady in white on the mantelpiece and said, "I'd like to spend Shabbat with Bertha." An inspired half-truth. Her cousin, Bertha Rott, lived across town on the other side of the river and the university. She was engaged to a student at the Jewish seminary, a boy her father approved of partly because of his knowledge of Torah, partly because of his connections to one of the old families of the Frankfurt community. But it was another Bertha—Bertha Teilheimer, leader of the Zionist youth group, that Hannah had in mind.

Edith, who was pushing potatoes around on her plate, caught on immediately. Her eyes flicked between Hannah and their father, her mouth twisted up in a smirk. Eliezer continued to chew chopped liver and challah and to wipe crumbs with a nervous hand from his stiff, black moustache.

"I'll stay over Sunday. I'll be home...."

"Yes, yes, fine." Eliezer waved his napkin at her.

There was not usually much talk at the Friday-night table unless Eliezer initiated it himself. He would aim his voice above his daughters' heads and at the tender-eyed woman on the mantelpiece. Sometimes he told jolly stories about the farmers who still came to his warehouse to buy grain sacks and cider barrels. Mostly he ranted. Not about the socialists anymore, since they'd been cleared off the streets with a speed that took even Eliezer aback. No, nowadays he heaped his scorn mainly upon Hitler's shameless louts and upon the secular Zionists. He had nothing against a return to Zion, but the wrong kind of Jews were returning. "Socialists with Stars of David on their chests.... Defilers of the Sabbath."

That evening, though, Eliezer was content to rail in silence, his lips twitching, his eyes smouldering with grievances. Hannah's shoulders sank back down from where they'd jumped up around her neck. She'd been hunching like a hen again, she realized. Something her father noticed and hated. She wanted to devote herself to the delicious roast potatoes with caraway seeds, but became alarmed once more when she glanced at Edith. Her sister was frowning and muttering at her plate, mouthing expressions of disdain, in perfect parody of their father. *"Lumpenpack...* scoundrels," she scolded the untouched potatoes and peas.

Hannah kicked her under the table. "Stop it," she mouthed. Edith's lips twisted into a half smile, part apology, part defiance.

"Edith, for heaven's sake, eat," Hannah said out loud.

"You're getting worse and worse. How can you expect to fill out if you don't eat?"

She said this almost by rote. The kind of words she'd been repeating day after day for years, since childhood. Hannah knew, of course, that Edith didn't expect to fill out. Her sister was convinced she was destined to be a runt and held to this view with what seemed to be perverse satisfaction. At fourteen she still had the same difficulty with food that she'd had as a baby, indifferent at best, squeamish over anything that was the least bit unfamiliar or not part of her short list of acceptable fodder. If anything, her fastidiousness had become worse. Often, she regarded her plate at mealtimes with anger and loathing. She didn't merely flatten and rearrange her mound of turnips. She stabbed at it and plunked over forkfuls onto Hannah's plate as if ridding herself of a burden. Often now, too, whispering her father's repertoire of insults during dinner, she mocked him, mocked herself, walked the thin edge of catastrophe.

She'd become odd. She practised what she called her disappearing act, standing close to walls, sitting so still in a corner of a room that people walked in and out without noticing her. Meanwhile, she watched everyone else with eyes ancient as a cat's. She roamed the city by herself in the coat with over-long sleeves that made her look even more waiflike and pathetic than she already was. Scattered on the dresser of the bedroom they shared, Hannah found tram ticket stubs for routes into suburbs where the family knew no-one.

"What on earth were you doing there?" Hannah asked, but Edith's face closed up in silence.

"It's not safe these days to wander about like that. Don't you know what's going on out there on the streets?"

And Edith's inevitable answer: "Who'd want to bother with little old me?"

Hannah worried, but she lost patience too, and sometimes Edith's disappearing act was most effective because

Hannah forgot all about her. It wasn't as it used to be when they were children. When Edith was a baby, Hannah hovered about the crib, sang her favourite songs to the pale, grublike infant that stared and sucked its fist at her. Edith would cry, not loudly but steadily, with eyes shut tight. Gertrude the nursemaid would seize her from the cradle and stuff a fat red forefinger into the baby's mouth to stop the noise. Hannah, five years old, took baby Edith onto her lap along with the knitted bedjacket that their mother used to wear and that was still kept laid out on the bed in Frau Fuchs' old room. A fine cream-coloured wool from before the war, smelling faintly of eau-de-cologne. Warm to the touch. Hannah wrapped the sleeves around Edith's neck.

"Mother loves you even if you're a small and miserable package," Hannah cooed. She piped, "*Hänschen klein...ging allein*...Little Hansie, went out alone, into the wide, wide world."

Their mother was dead, no longer locked into that narrow, wasted body in the bedroom. Her spirit had been freed to spread throughout the house, infusing itself into tile stove, cuckoo clock, feather comforters—anything that didn't have their father's stamp upon it. During Frau Fuchs' long illness, Hannah was rarely allowed into the sick-room but she knew that the woman on the bed was shrinking like story-book Kaspar who wouldn't eat his dinner. In her dreams Hannah was terrified of crushing her cricket-sized mother under her own ungainly duck feet. Puny Edith had something of the diminished Frau Fuchs about her. In Edith's small, serious, old-man's face and limp neck, their mother's suffering was reborn.

At one time, Edith had craved her father's attention. When very young she would charge into the library and tumble at his feet while he stood at morning prayers. Wrapped in his prayer shawl, his gaze remained fixed on the prayer book held stiffly before him and his voice droned on, the words like stones churning round and round in his mouth. Hannah would hurry into the room to pull Edith away and it was Hannah who would catch the irate glare, the jerk of his chin indicating the door. Nowadays no-one interrupted his prayers or his tirades, directed at the Nazi broadcasts on the radio and the secular Jewish press.

Dinner was over. It had proceeded through its various courses, mercifully, without outbursts. The endless Blessings after Meals had also come to an end. Their father was in his study and Hannah was able to pack her knapsack in anticipation of the excursion ahead. She was going off with her youth group into the mountains. Two glorious days of hiking, singing, dancing around the campfire, serious discussions about politics and religion that everyone could take part in, even an ignoramus like herself. How had she lived before the *Blau-Weiss*, the Zionist youth group? It had been mere existence, not a life. A tearful daily struggle with her secretarial job at the Warburg Bank. She had no talent for the work and had the job only because of the intercession of an uncle with connections. She had tried to learn to type. Her blunt fingers thumped down on the keyboard making a cluster of keys fly up and lock together in a frozen embrace. Mistakes in every sentence. Or gouged out empty spaces where the keys had smacked down too hard. She saw sly smirks on the other girls' faces while their cool white hands danced, and her old inner voices started up: "Clumsy cow. Worthless. Useless." If only the supervisor would notice her agony and give her another task or show her the door. It was a busy time. A run on accounts one day, a flurry of deposits the next. People wavering. Waiting to see what the regime would do next.

Then she encountered the *Blau-Weissers* and the humiliations of the bank no longer mattered. It was Bertha Teilheimer who brought her to the Reform synagogue to hear a young rabbi deliver a talk about the Jewish homeland. Forbidden territory, this building with the wide steps, the

Romanesque arches, the organ pipes glimmering under stained-glass windows—what her father called the temple of sin. She didn't care for services, even the Reform brand, but she was happy for an excuse to tread unholy ground. Throughout the talk Bertha kept Hannah's arm tucked under her own and squeezed it when the rabbi made his salient points. She needn't have. The moment he began to speak a veil lifted and Hannah saw the world in clear, sharp relief. Of course, of course. The Zionists had everything. Not just ideals of equality and brotherhood, but a perfect, unborn country and a final answer to the Jewish question, ending the circular arguments about whether one was German of Jewish faith or Jew of German citizenship or total alien.

An unborn country across the wide, blue Mediterranean, far from the tired old hatreds of Europe. Far from her father's house.

After the talk, the young people—girls and boys she knew from school days—formed a big circle and danced the *hora* to music from a scratchy record on the gramophone. Although Hannah couldn't quite manage the pattern of steps, it didn't matter, her legs flew. She leapt into the whirl of motion, the stamp of feet, the intoxicating charge into the centre of the ring.

As Hannah paused while rummaging in her drawer for matching stockings, she became aware of a mournful sound from inside the great armoire—a stifled warbling that raised the hairs on the back of her neck. She yanked open the door, making the whole closet rattle.

"Edith, you gave me a fright. Why didn't you say something? And why can't you play something more cheerful? You sound like a graveyard."

There was Edith, crouched on the floor of the armoire under the clothes, her recorder on her knees.

"I'm trying to be quiet. And it was a cheerful song. It

was the Miller's Wandering Song. To help you get into the mood for your trip."

Hannah hated when Edith played her music in the closet. For some reason it set her teeth on edge. And yet she knew she wasn't being fair because where else could Edith play on the Sabbath? Their father's study was only two rooms away.

"Come out and talk to me instead of hiding in your cave. Anyway, I have to get in there and find my blue skirt."

Edith raised an arm and plucked the blue skirt off its hanger as if plucking an apple. She unfolded her limbs and emerged, blinking in the room's electric light. Then she sat on her bed, arms around her knees, watching, while Hannah searched for missing underpants, a spare handkerchief, her good wool vest. Hannah found herself humming under her breath as she packed. "Oh the miller loves to wander, loves to wander." The stirring old tune lodged itself in her head.

"Two whole days in the mountains," she exulted, and then stopped with a stab of guilt. Edith had to go to school. Edith would be alone with their father.

"You know you really should join the *Blau-Weissers*. There's a group of youngsters your age. If only you'd give it a try."

For answer, Edith jumped up and began to cavort Hassidic style around the room, arms in the air, eyes half closed. She sang a satirical song in Yiddish that Hannah remembered from her own school days.

"Oh how fine it will be when the Messiah comes
We will build a land out of paper
We will all march together
Oi, yoi, yoi, yoi"

Edith bleated out the words and the "oi yois" in a high, nasal voice, so convincing that Hannah couldn't help but hoot with laughter.

"Stop it," she said, between gasps. "You've got it all wrong. That's the old, anti-Zionist propaganda. For one thing it's not mostly eastern Jews anymore. There's lots of us Germans. More of us every day."

But Edith could not be cajoled or reasoned with. She laughed off Hannah's urgings and finally she said, "They don't want a scrawny mouse like me. I'm not built to be a pioneer."

"No, no. We're both going to Palestine together," said Hannah, but it was hard to sound convincing while looking at Edith's stick arms and legs and her pale, pinched face.

A tap at the door. It was Tilly, the maid, come to switch off the light, one of the innumerable forms of labour forbidden on the Sabbath. The two sisters undressed in the dark, snuggled under their feather beds and immediately Hannah was off in a dream about the journey to come. She saw herself arm in arm with Bertha, marching down a country road under a broad and brilliant sky.

Hannah jumped out of bed into a room still submerged in night. It was part of her plot to slip out before dawn, before her father was up and would see her with her knapsack. Edith would make up a story about why she'd left early. Or perhaps he wouldn't ask, too intent on rushing out the door and scurrying to the little backroom prayer house where he met with his cohorts to usher in the Sabbath. She dressed as quietly as she could, but Edith stirred, muttered something and stuck a leg out of the blankets.

"Shh, Edie, go back to sleep."

"I have to get to school."

"It's not six o'clock yet."

"I have to sneak out with my books. I forgot to leave them yesterday."

"Oh, for heaven's sakes, Edith."

Every Saturday, the dilemma of the schoolbooks. It was

the law of the Sabbath that Edith carry nothing, not even a handkerchief, when she went out of the house. It was the law of the land that she go to school on Saturdays. Both laws must be obeyed. Eliezer could see no reason why not, even in these days of uncertainty and trouble when it was best not to draw attention to oneself. "In every generation there are those who rise up against us," Eliezer quoted from the Haggadah with sour triumph. And yet generations of Fuchses and Rotts and Goldsteins had managed. Orthodox children had gone to state schools to receive a decent, thorough German education while keeping the Sabbath. They refrained from writing and carrying on Saturdays and of course were often tormented for it, but some teachers had been most understanding. Eliezer spoke fondly of his own master, Herr Kraus, a retired cavalry officer, who appreciated the extra discipline that the Jew had to bear, the unquestioning obedience to orders from on High. For years, Edith had a Shabbas goy—a Christian schoolmate who had carried her books on the Sabbath, since Eliezer would not allow any of the non-observing Jewish children to do it. But this year the girl had announced, chin in the air, that a pure-blooded German must not serve as mule for the Jew.

"Please Papa. Relax the rules," Hannah had urged.

Eliezer had stared at her as if she'd lost her senses. He had his own solution. Quite simple really. A cupboard in the school basement where the janitor would allow Edith to store her book satchel overnight on Fridays and pick it up in the morning. The janitor was kind enough. No-one else even had to know about this special arrangement. The only problem was that Edith kept forgetting. She brought back her bag on Fridays and Saturday morning had to endure a scene. Hannah doubted that Edith would now creep quietly with her out of the house. She would probably rouse Eliezer, and his wrath would pour down on them both.

"Give me the bag, Edith. I'll pass by the school on my way to the train."

"But it's out of your way. You don't have to do that."

"Yes, yes. Get back into bed."

Edith mumbled her thanks and pulled the covers up around her ears. She hated the cold, especially the chill of early morning. Book-bag on one shoulder, knapsack on the other, Hannah slipped out of the dark apartment, down the stone stairway and into the street where a fog smelling of river slime and coal dust greeted her.

The central train station rose massive and still in the early morning light, the new flag with its twisted-arm emblem motionless over the portal. But stepping inside Hannah was embraced by the familiar boom and bustle that always drove her heart a little faster. Her group was gathered on Platform 7 where the train for Waldenburg already waited, snorting steam. Like herself, each carried a knapsack or bundle, each was dressed for the mountains in warm jacket and sturdy shoes. Some held walking-sticks which they pumped in their eagerness against the platform floor. There was Hugo, his face deep brown and scratched from the farm-work training he'd already begun in preparation for his new life in Palestine. He planned to be off before the new year, to "redeem the land," as they said in the movement. He glanced at Hannah, a quick, warm look, and Lisel nudged Hilda, it all happened in a moment. Hannah tried, but could not smile back in the open, friendly and nononsense way that would have been the right answer to the nudging. Neck stiff, she moved to the edge of the group aware of the largeness of her hands and a tiny dart twitching inside her. She calmed herself by surveying the platform scene.

A young porter stood nearby, one hand clasped around the handle of his tipped up trundle cart, the other hand holding a cigarette that he seemed to have forgotten. A thin stream of smoke drifted up from between his fingers. He stared, eager and curious, at the cluster of *Blau-Weissers* before him, as if he wished he could join in their camaraderie. No-one else seemed to notice him or the swastika that winked from his lapel. No armband or brown shirt, just the small square of red and black felt being distributed at rallies. He continued to gaze at the centre of the group trying to catch someone's eye, to be included through a friendly smile or wave, she was sure of that. How often she herself had stared with pained longing at a cluster of people before she had found her place with the *Blau-Weissers*.

Would it dawn on him who they were? Would that soft, foolish longing harden into something quite different? She almost wished that her friends would reveal themselves with an outlandish word or gesture. But of course they did not. If they spoke of movement affairs or used a Yiddish phrase it was *sotte voce*, speaking below the hiss of engines. The porter continued to stare and smile out of his turnip face at fine German youth on an outing. For a moment, they all seemed frozen in their roles like figures on a play-bill; no-one had any substance. And then, the blast of the train whistle, the press of bodies boarding the train, the city behind them and the gently rising countryside ahead.

They slept at a farm outside the quaint and ancient resort town of Waldenberg. There was some question as to whether the youth hostels on the mountain trails had become restricted and it seemed safer to use the farmer's place —he was glad of the payment—as a base. Above the farm, hidden from view by the thick forest, the great mountain range stretched for 500 miles along the German-Czech border, spilling into both countries without discrimination. Hannah had been on some of the lesser slopes during school day-trips but never before had slept in mountain air, or spent so much time in the presence of the giants.

They hiked along the trails, single file or three abreast as the path widened, their voices threaded together in song.

"*Anu holchim ba regel....* We go by foot, *hoppa, hoppa, hoppa, hey*," they shouted in Hebrew. Quickly exhausting

90

their Hebrew repertoire, they launched into one after another of the old German wandering songs. "The Miller
Loves to Wander," "Frankfurt I Must Leave You," "He
Who Wanders with Purest Heart." In the evening they
returned to the farm to cook potatoes and sausages in a
campfire in the open field. At night, the girls retired into
the barn, while the boys stayed outside beside the hay ricks.
There were more hopeful looks from Hugo, but Hannah
stayed close to Bertha and the girls, content with the vague
and pleasant glow created by the distance between them.

And yet, and yet. There were times when Hannah's skin
prickled with frustration, when she wanted to jump up and
run from the campfire circle. Discussions and debates about
strategy. How to comport oneself in the new Germany?
How to win over the masses of unaffiliated Jews, embarrassed by talk of a Jewish homeland? And how to answer
the criticism that they were merely playing into Hitler's
hands by encouraging emigration to a new "ghetto" in the
desert? The talk went on and on during their final evening
together. It flared up, died down, began anew, arguments
piling on top of one another. It broke the spell of the
mountains and left Hannah weary and restless. She lay in
the hayloft that night, listening to the snuffle of horses below and couldn't sleep. The thought of the journey home
next day gnawed at her. Too brief, too brief. Their time was
over before it had properly begun. Then it occurred to her
that if she wasn't ready to leave, she didn't have to. The
bank could do without her one more day. Before dawn she
left a note in Bertha's shoe. "I've gone for one last ramble,"
she wrote. "I'll catch the three o'clock train back to town.
Don't worry. I know my way."

She found the stairway leading from the road up the side of
the mountain, into the cold, dark embrace of the forest. Old
stone steps sunk into the mountain, slippery with moss.
Goethe walked here, did he not, tapping these very steps

with his cane? Eichendorf floated on the smell of fir, beech, birch and pine into one of his fairy stories. The hiking trail she wanted was marked with a stone pillar, the letters "S.K." for *Schneekoppe*—the highest peak of the range—engraved there, but she had to feel for them like a blind woman because of the fur of moss.

Trees blurred and billowed, their skirts danced in the breeze, branches touched. Each leaf took its turn on the wind, bowing to no partners. She walked and the old song sang in her head, the rhythm of the forest entered her feet.

"Das Wanderen ist des Muller's lust...." She hummed and then sang out loud. Her limbs thrummed with life, with the energy that can only come from walking. She drank in the air and the smell of pines.

After a time—she could not have said how long—she emerged from thick forest into low-growth alpine terrain. Below were lesser slopes, long deep valleys, meadows dotted with sheep, here and there a wisp of smoke, a strip of road. The breath of the giants swirled around her. Boulders lost their edges. Her hand disappeared when she stretched out her arm. Her feet found the trail though her eyes could barely see it and she went on and on in the mist.

At a bend in the path she stopped. A crow cawed and then it was silent. No wind, no sound except for the thump in her ears. The mist luminous, opaque and strange. Was someone there? Someone waiting with malicious intent? She held her breath. She strained to hear. Nothing. Nothing.

"Edith," she heard herself say out loud. "Edith."

Edith was in danger. She tried to dismiss the thought. She tried to conjure her sister, drifting home from school through the park along the river, clutching her book-bag by its cracked leather strap. With each step onwards a foreboding pressed against Hannah's heart. She turned back and hurried downwards although it seemed to her that whatever had happened—if something indeed had happened—she could do nothing. Only fret.

Edith was already home from the hospital when Hannah arrived back in town. Her arm was in a sling and half her face—the side on which her hair was parted and therefore more exposed—was greenish-blue and swollen.

"I look like one of those decadent modern paintings," she said in a dull, far-off voice while passing the hall mirror. But she said little else and Eliezer, too, was close-lipped, grim and distant. Hannah learned the most about what had happened from Tilly, in the kitchen. Edith had fallen out of the doorway of the Number 12 tram as it came hurtling around the road into Tauenzienplatz. Miraculously, she'd sustained only minor injuries. The doctor said she would soon be good as new again.

"Herr Fuchs could not understand what she was doing on a tram in the middle of the Sabbath," said Tilly, eyes wide with the horror of it. "He was called away from his afternoon Torah study."

"A terrible accident," Tilly hastened to add when Hannah stared at her.

At first Hannah thought it was the Hitler Youth. You didn't just fall out of a tram. Someone should at least tell the *Centralverein*, the general community council, Hannah thought. These cases should at least be documented. But Eliezer glared at her when she made the suggestion and shook his head in disgust.

"And what about you," he growled. "I suppose you want me to believe you were kidnapped by the SA. Transported to the mountains!" He turned away as if unable to bear the sight of her and marched toward the coat stand. "Give my regards to cousin Bertha," he shouted as he slammed the front door.

After he left, the apartment became still and oppressive. How heavy and useless the familiar old furniture—massive dining-room table, brocade couch—appeared to Hannah after her walk among the pines. The living-room was filled with a sad, grey light and from the grandfather clock in the

93

hallway came a hollow tick-tock and groan of metal. But although the living-room seemed empty, Edith was there, Hannah knew. The tired air, the listless drapes, spoke of her presence. Hannah waited a moment, then walked over to the windowsill.

"Edith," she said.

"Yes," came a toneless voice from behind the drapes. Hannah pulled aside the folds of fabric and there sat Edith in the wide bay window, resting her bandaged arm on her drawn-up knees. The undamaged side of her face was turned to the light and was smooth and blank as carved stone. Hannah lowered herself beside her and began to pass her fingertips, as lightly as she could, over the outer layer of her sister's hair. Her big hand trembled as she touched, afraid of its weight, of the bruises hidden beneath the hairline. She took a deep breath.

"Did you jump or were you pushed?"

"Jumped."

"Oh, Edie, why, why?"

But Edith could only shrug and make a self-mocking grimace.

"Edith, Edele," Hannah crooned. "Promise me you'll never do this again. Promise me you'll come to the *Blau-Weiss*. And next year, after I've saved up the money, we'll go to Palestine together, you and me. We'll take the ship from Trieste across the Mediterranean Sea and every day it will be warmer and warmer. And then we will be with the Haverim, the comrades. And you'll get sun-tanned and strong. Maybe even fat."

Edith smiled as she leaned her head against Hannah's shoulder.

"You old donkey," she said.

On the street below, automobiles snorted and trams rattled by. Someone's hammer rang against a nail. The newsboy bawled out the headlines in voice that was hoarse but full of new-found zeal.

DARRYL WHETTER

Sitting Up

Danny has always hated flies. He slowly but firmly shuts the half-open bathroom door and reaches for a magazine. *Thwap!* Worst thing about summer. *Thwap!* The fly escapes upward and buzzes moronically along the ceiling. Danny will wait, a cylinder of *Popular Science* tight in hand. *Maclean's, Men's Health, Canadian Consumer,* a whole basket of them in the corner—his father's "Reading Room." Danny is eleven, just old enough to hate the phrase and cringe every time Perry uses it when friends are over. The hidden side of the white wicker basket is dimpled with dents from Danny's occasionally enraged foot.

This particular magazine has been sitting on top of the toilet tank for about a week, quietly flaunting "Tomorrow's Soldier," wireless speakers and the latest on-board computer. *Thwap!* Impatience rises up Danny's back like a fast spider. Stepping up onto the edge of the tub he holds onto the shower-curtain rod with one hand and guns the ceiling repeatedly with the other. A curved strip of the cover photo stares back at him. The camouflaged Nintendo soldier bends sharply at the neck with every smack.

"Danny, you okay in there?" Perry asks from the other side of the door.

"No problem, Dad!"

Thwap!

"Just a—" *Thwap! Thwap!* "—fly."

Ruff.

Salsa is apparently ambling along at Perry's side, quick to speak up at any sign of civil unrest.

Thwap. Thwap.

Ruff. Ruff.

"What?!" Perry asks, raising his voice over muffled smacks and collie protests.

"Fly, Dad, fly!" Danny yells back, all the while giving it

the home-try across the shiny white ceiling and along the yellow walls. Minutes ago, when Danny was scalding his fingers under the taps (in too much of a rush to shut the door), Perry was off in a book.

"Just checking," Perry answers, dropping the last syllable as he walks off.

Salsa's tags jangle and fade through the house like casual music.

"It's his third visit in an hour-and-a-half. Really." Rebecca's grip on her watering can tightens slightly as she stares over at the man she has begun to think of more often as *her husband* than as *Perry*. Her other hand repeatedly rolls and releases the clump of assorted leaves she has just gathered from the living-room's numerous plants. "What do you need, a signed confession?"

Perry looks up from his latest hardcover, giving her a probationary look both of them know he feels is beneath him.

"Privacy Rebecca, it's his right."

No longer able to see himself in the bathroom mirror, Danny had been trying to stay the pendulum of his vision with an opened hot-water tap. The itch of his fingers removed the focus from his eyes as if focus was the pit of a small fruit—cherries, olives, grapes. Hot water—the clarity of pain, the quick anchor in Danny's ken. A knot of white light ties itself beautifully for just a few seconds each time he pushes his itching, weeping fingers forward into the cylinder of hot running water. Lately he's been staring into the chrome faucet when the heat starts biting too closely, needling through the edge of troublesome eczema to wrap each finger in strips of growing pain. He gives the last few seconds to this series of tiny, distorted reflections in the chrome faucet, six Dannies looming and head-heavy like rock-video heroes.

Looking up this time he'd noticed the fly in the mirror, a dumb black dot on the wall behind him. Shutting off the tap he reached for the nearby magazine without shifting his gaze. His wet fingers made several paper puddles as he rolled *Popular Science* into a glossy baton. Turning and shutting the door, Danny narrowed the field of play. This one had been in the house for days.

Thwap! Gut-wet, the fly's body sticks to the slick paper. Danny knocks the corpse into the discrete peach garbage can and tosses the magazine on top of the rest. Walking off, he hears the magazine unroll like a yawn.

Last Saturday Danny had walked back into his bedroom to the sight of a fly rummaging over his soiled blue jockeys. Last Saturday he'd jerked off for the ninth time and then gone to wash his hands, staring himself in the face. Eight times more than he'd planned. Danny Carruthers, initiate in white knots.

Skin problems as long as he can remember. When he throws off the bed covers there's a blizzard of dust in the strong morning sun. *Dyshydrosis:* patches of his young skin drier than any old man's, elephant elbows and dusty, purple knees. *Eczema*: a rash he knows in every stage, the small white arrival, the red territorial ambitions and cursing yellow fade. And then their passionate, incestuous affair: *dyshydrotic eczema*, a combination of scales and pustules on the fingers of his right hand, a series of fissures, flakes and swellings that arrive in under 24 hours and linger for as long as two weeks. But he's never had anything like this new frosty patch on his left thigh.

In this past year Rebecca has seen her boy starting to shield his right hand, curling the fingers inwards, using his hands less as he speaks and pointing with his left despite his right-handedness. Back in the early years, Grades 1 and 2,

98

she couldn't imagine Danny caring at all. He would speak of his *rash*, or his *cream*, but otherwise do boy things. He only felt deprived for not being able to have bubble-baths.

The lesions meant he was prone to infection and little "topical viruses." *Impetigo* once a season. One time the little gold islands sprang up over his whole face. He was ordered home from school but didn't feel sick at all. TV and books in the mornings, afternoons outside. An only child adept at self-amusement.

Danny, fly-killer, walks from the downstairs bathroom and passes by the glowing living-room.

"'Bout time for bed isn't it?" Perry calls out without looking up from his book, his forehead lit up blue from Rebecca's distant TV.

"Going," Danny replies flatly as he walks past the living-room and his concerned, news-hungry parents. "Night."

"Goodnight," they both chime amidst reports of mar-shalling troops and failing US polls.

F L Y. Danny traces the letters over and over again in his head while climbing the stairs. Danny the Fly.

Rebecca hears the upstairs sink start to run and waits for the creak of the medicine chest to open and close. She used to enjoy knowing what her men were doing in the house by the noises they made. Thankfully Salsa's always been a quiet dog. Rebecca suspects she has begun to hear other sounds. All his life she's heard Danny scratching, awake or asleep, day or night—her boy the noisy dreamer. And sud-denly these private noises.

This morning she vowed to say something. Anticipating jokes, Perry's curt response was even less co-operative than she'd expected. Perry has a bad habit that makes worse of his bad jokes. He cooks them up months before or after an event. This is good in some ways, Rebecca has told herself, shows he's thinking. "Adolescence," Perry starts with a pause, "from bathroom to bedroom to car." He's been working on the big ones since Danny was born. Buying his son the first pack of condoms (a modest three): *Put a bag on that bugger.* University graduation: *Nothing left to do now but bail you out of jail.* Perry'll dust off the same joke again and again even when he knows his audience has heard them before. A man with no sense of expiry, a back of the fridge rooter. He's recently been doing the rounds with, "I love making cappuccino, it's like getting to use power tools and blow bubbles in my milk at the same time." Perry Carruthers, man of truisms.

Lemony geranium leaf in hand, Rebecca's ears keep ringing. *Privacy Rebecca, it's his right.*

Danny gives up brushing his teeth with his left hand and stares at his war-torn right. Its ugliness still amazes him. How does he get through the day? How can he actually get used to the pocked, pink base, the cracks and lacerations that sediment themselves like dry, flaked mud, and the perpetual rainbow of infection? He only risks flossing one week out of eight.

"Since when did you stop liking hamburgers?" Rebecca recently asked as Danny sat spearing dry fries with a fork. She hasn't made sense of his recent switch to eating pizza or even fried chicken with a knife and fork. She has sat wiping grease from her fingers, oblivious and questioning.

When Danny's fingers are this bad everything seems to make them worse—writing, gloves, water, soap, the spit and toothpaste that can run down a brush handle. He suspends hand-washing, dreads every crap, and reduces face-washing to once a day, bed-time. Masturbating? Skin rubbing skin? Good, that will help him quit.

This time it's so bad Danny is washing his face with just one hand, feeling like a sudden amputee each night.

"Jim Abbott."

Danny looks up to Perry standing in the bathroom doorway.

"That one-handed pitcher I was telling you about—Jim Abbott. Plays for Philadelphia."

Perry smiles and nods encouragingly at Dan's hands as if everything can now resume.

"Thanks Dad," Danny replies, dismissing his father as he bends toward one handful of water, closing his eyes for an insufficient splash.

Crossing his bedroom in darkness, Danny reaches for the light on his headboard. This is the sort of thing he likes about his father—Danny has grown up with plenty of lights to read by. Standing in his little blue underwear he stares from his thigh into the mirror and back again. Nothing, just smooth skin. Tracing the thigh with a delicate fingertip he tries to locate some discernible edge to the patch, fingering for a quicksand shore. The dresser-top mirror in his room is far too large, sprawling along half a wall: the sort of thing he hates about his mother.

Danny reaches for the golf pencil tucked between the mattresses and traces over this invisible, palm-sized patch on his thigh.

F L Y

He traces the letters neatly, filling the patch of skin as if his hip were the left side of a page and his knee the right. The pencil leaves no mark. It's only the point he needs. Eventually, budding ironist, Danny'll use a dead pen.

Climbing into bed slowly, Danny swings the leg up as if it were locked in a cast. Last year when Peter Jenkins broke his leg he was showered with attention. Mrs. Billings would let friends stay inside at recess with him and even permitted the occasional Jenkins Obstacle Course of desks and chairs. Sarah Miller gave Peter a whole box of wide markers to keep in his desk so people would be able to sign and draw over his cast in colour. By the next day Sarah and

Becky had taken up two whole lunch hours drawing up and down Peter: clouds and a rainbow, a bike, and their two faces like a signature on the inside of the ankle. Danny's get-well hello had been mostly covered over by a row of rainbow purple.

Danny draws up the blankets slowly, careful not to disturb the thigh. Proudly reaching for his book he looks down one last time before lowering the sheets. He had only dented the skin for the letters, not one superfluous stroke. When he wakes in the morning F L Y will have risen in a neat, tough line of hives: *dermigraphia*'s the latest. Setting *Sword of Thieves* aside he rolls a sock onto each hand and reaches for the light, waiting like a bird in the oven.

Danny knows he's starting to tick, a veritable clock and calendar of skin. His fingers are smooth and everybody-pink for a couple of weeks before another blitzkrieg of swelling and itching. Some try to ignore it, others question (sympathetically or not) or offer local advice—St. John's Oil, camomile tea and soap, aloe vera. The prescription creams, one stinking goop or another, can only keep the swelling and itching at bay. Healing happens or doesn't. Danny has come to watch the colours of his skin like a sailor the sky, smoothness and health sought like a horizon.

All of this is trouble enough, and now these hives. At first he noticed them helplessly, dense and frozen in his skin like bubbles in ice, immovable and repugnant. Every morning he'd stare down his smooth, fruit-skin chest to his thigh, back and forth in the too-wide mirror, hoping they would vanish with a *poof* if he stared long enough. Why this inch and not that one? Why do his dad's whiskers grow only halfway up on his face? One night Danny reached for a nearby pencil to poke for numbness and sensations, just like doctors had done to him. The next morning's hives weren't lines but spots, poke signatures.

It's no sweat at all for Danny to call the cab on time. The day started with a $20 bill from his mother tucked under her list of a few suggested questions for Dr. Schwartz. The bill rested in his pocket all morning, its outline occasionally traced by an undamaged fingertip.

Stepping out of the taxi Danny flips the cabby back a loony before shutting the door, saying "Thanks man," as if it's nothing.

Settling into the waiting-room he reaches for *People* and its assortment of low-cut dresses, trying not to stare at the older man in work clothes with a bubbly, dark purple stain consuming half of his face.

Sitting in front of Dr. Schwartz's wide desk, Danny stares past her and out the windows beyond. She murmurs a greeting while reading a file. The building across the street is almost identical to this one, and beside it another, vertical blinds and fluorescent lights taking up an overcast sky. Painted letters fill the ground-floor windows.

"Okay Danny, let's see this leg," Dr. Schwartz announces, looking up with a trained smile.

Danny is motionless longer than he'd like. Stupidly he reaches down to his ankles, tugging at his pant-leg to see if it will rise all the way up above his knee. Finally he stands and undoes his pants. The top of her desk is even with his young thigh. A pewter-framed family portrait stares at Danny's F L Y thigh and the window measures his dick.

"Um-hum. Hop up on the table behind you please, Danny."

Danny tries to raise his pants during the few steps to the examining-table, bending and shuffling, all the while aware of the powder-blue raisin of his jockeyed rump and the room's professional, impatient eyes. Dr. Schwartz takes a few long strides in expensive shoes and waits for him beside the bed-like table, one hand resting on a metal stirrup. The wax-paper covering crinkles with every shift and Danny can feel a dent forming from the heat of his ass. Dave wouldn't have to do this. Or Kyle. Chris, Scott, or Matt.

"Mmm-hmm," Schwartz exhales more than she says, reaching into a jacket pocket for a magnifying glass. Gripping Danny's whole thigh just above the knee she leans down toward the patch. Cars honk and start at the intersection. Her other large hand comes down, mid-thigh, as both pull the skin and roll it around the muscle. Her hip presses against his other knee.

Say something, please!

Danny's little fellow is starting to rise, pitching his jockeys into a glaring blue tent. He hauls his folded arms in tighter. A hand on his thigh. A magnifying glass on his hives.

Salsa's been hit by a car. Salsa's been hit by a car.

"Dermigraphia," Dr. Schwartz says conclusively, already looking back to desk and file.

In the second it takes her to cross behind her desk, Danny hops off the table, hauling up his pants before his feet hit the ground. Snapping the dome at his waist he thinks again of how much he hates these pants, their sick, khaki hue, their stiff, scratchy feel. His penis is subsiding mercifully and his mother still buys his clothes.

The doctor taps a pen down the file.

"You don't have any other patches like this one?"

"No."

"Has it gotten any bigger?"

Dr. Schwartz dismisses Danny with an antihistamine to bring down the swelling.

The skin of his thigh has become a template of hives. Localized pressure, a thumbprint say, or a thin medical instrument, becomes embossed in a tough line of hives eight hours later. Traitors hide in his thigh, knots of patience awaiting one command. *Rise.* Winks and nods circulate in blood and brain. Danny leaves the office sorry for every paraplegic.

"Danny! What have you done to your leg?"

Rebecca practically drops the cereal bowl she had been reaching to set in front of him.

"Nothing."

"What do you mean nothing?!"

Hauling Danny's chair out, Rebecca pulls the leg of his *L'il Walkers* up to reveal H A N D written in puffed-up hives. His friends all wear high-cut soccer or surf shorts. She thought Danny'd want something longer. Her chin starts quivering.

"Excuse me," Danny snaps, brushing her hand aside, adjusting his seat and reaching for the Raisin Bran.

Her chin keeps going and her lips form and reform a silent *P* as a lost sergeant in her skull shouts *Perry, Perry* into the din. Turning, eventually, with the gawkiness of an industrial crane, Rebecca looks down, conscious of her nightgown and the bareness of her collarbones.

"You cannot do that," she manages to say with two scoops between them.

"Doesn't make a difference," Danny mumbles, crunching and pretending to read the box.

"You'll only make things worse."

"No I won't," he replies clearly, looking directly into her face, "Dr. Schwartz told me nothing will make it worse. It's from the inside. It just is."

"I don't want you doing this to yourself."

"Why?"

"Danny—that's disgusting."

"No Mom, hives are disgusting, eczema is disgusting." Glaring up at her, a spoonful of milk in his left hand.

Danny isn't aware of the steroids in his cream and he doesn't realize track stars are impotent. His *cream*, his *rash*. The little squat pharmacy jars have changed over the years from dark brown glass to slick white plastic and the type-written labels have been replaced with laser-printed efficiency. Bethamethazone, betnovate, betademia: more steroids than a football locker room.

These medicinal creams are smeared with hope of reversing the red tide. Increasingly familiar with this itchy time in his body, Danny is beginning to understand *costs*. The steroids which allegedly reduce the swelling and mitigate the itching also thin the skin and suppress the local immune system. The tough fissures that end an outbreak are made susceptible to greater infection by the very substance he thinks is helping. The fingers torn raw by nails, cloth or scalding water now sediment and flake, left weak and brittle by cortisone.

Occasionally Danny worries the patches are actually his fear being calibrated on his skin, as if the red advance up fingers and hands is the mercury in a thermometer of regret. It *is* scaring him, not the pain or itching, the lint-filled fissures or yellow, candied crystals that harden over the lesions, but healing. Danny is most afraid of a healthy hand. The light whimsical departure that eventually, arbitrarily, follows the red military arrival is so much harder to understand. If one day is sickness and the next health, where does healing wait?

Danny flips through his robotics calendar, nervous of any Tuesday, wondering whether August 28th or, yikes, October 2nd, will be good or bad days. Turning back to July he studies the fresh notes of his recent thigh-diary: 14 July H A N D, 16 July H E R, 17 July H E R B. Reaching for his little pencil he jots down tonight's, M A P, in the perfect calendar square, studying it like a nervous engineer before taking pencil to thigh.

"Dermimappia," Danny jokes aloud to the morning-keen dog, holding up his shorts to show Salsa the M A P of hives complete with a dotted trail and an X marking the spot.

Salsa doesn't lick Danny when his fingers are bad even though she's been walking slobber for years. Rebecca eventually read an article claiming licking was an act of aggression, especially because Salsa was female. By then it was too late, old dogs. Compared to Perry or visiting friends and relatives, Rebecca rarely gets the tongue.

Locking his bike in the usual place, Danny walks the few remaining blocks to the arcade.

"Danny, whassup?"

Danny returns Nathan's greeting with a nod, hoping this not-too-close friend won't try to shake hands. It's that time of the cycle and Danny is wearing long-sleeved shirts to the arcade, learning to take the heat and trying to ignore the sting of sweat in his series of open sores.

Dropping in his quarters, Danny starts up *StreetWarrior*. High-kick, low-punch, shoulder-throw. He stops feeling his sneakers, the various blips and phasers drop away from his ears. The worse his fingers are the higher his score. Round-house, speed-bag. Danny knows the distance between skin and bone. There is no time to scratch when he's ducking a simulated barrel or wielding a digital chain. Danny cracks an audible jaw and advances to the next stage, enjoying the screen's devoted glow all over his face.

StreetChick clips Danny repeatedly with a series of high kicks to the nose before *Warlock* buries both meaty fists in his kidneys. Danny catches the jump button with the mid-knuckle of his left hand, springing to a park bench before fully extending a leg into the base of *Warlock's* spine, earning extra points and increased speed. Nathan comes over at these sounds of victory.

"Whassup?"

In arcades, no-one makes eye contact when they speak. Everything that matters is onscreen, even the reflections of their young, bursting heads. Danny doesn't acknowledge his weeping fingers. A clear liquid, neither blood nor pus, shines up out of the rounder lesions, quickly yellowing if he presses it into paper or a white T-shirt. *Mainline's* coming at him with a broken bottle. *Ratzo's* got a baseball bat. Danny drops another quarter for extended life and watches his virtual chest heave. The longer he plays the more he'll scratch as soon as he's two steps out of the arcade. The warrior's focus.

Working the kick button into each member of *The Red Leathers*, Danny steals a glance at Nathan's spectatorial face, wondering if this guy with better clothes and a more expensive skateboard can see the mess on his fingers, the street-fighting glow reflected in a series of small red puddles.

Regions of Danny's brain admit he shouldn't scratch. He's been doing it all his life on any surface he can find. The accurate, severe edge of a rivet in the corner pocket of his jeans, good for a deft scrape in public. The tall worker of an open cupboard door, the wobbly, giving abrasion of the edge of his mattress, or the dangerous, desperate-measures of the hard, low-pile rug in his room.

Nathan doesn't say a word. Even if he is admiring Danny's every kick and gouge, he's still ultimately waiting for Danny to take one too many in the ribs and go down panting. Success in a game is only ever failure delayed. Silence is the undisputed dialect of the arcade, respect and loathing slightly different gradations of a clenched jaw.

Quick Dragon ends Danny's game with a flurry of punches, up and down the mid-section, tossing his spent body onto the black spikes of a park fence before defiling it with pixelated spit.

"Nice game," Nathan claims with a world of effort as he slides his quarters in for the next round.

Still at the controls, Danny pretends to wipe his brow with one sleeve, surreptitiously patting his weeping fingers on the cloth he gathers. Using stick and buttons he enters D A N on the highscore list before banging the final buttons with the other sleeve to mop up the tiny infectious puddles they seemed designed to hold. 59,345. Fourth place, not bad at all.

Walking out into the glaring sun Danny's hands are already halfway into his pockets, fingers working up the hard seams of denim. Stooping to unlock his bike Danny's face presses close to his palimpsest thigh. Standing again he fishes for the golf pencil he has taken to carrying around in his pocket.

5 9 3 4 5 pressed into his waiting skin.

The pencil he took from his mother's golf-bag.

He'll grab a chocolate bar and ride around town, rising.

Home around five, Danny locks his bike and slips in through the back. The sounds of an argument stop him by the door.

"Only for the rough nights. Perry, he's ripping himself to shreds."

"Another drug?"

They're in the living-room, on the other side of the hall to Danny's cocked-ears.

"I'm only talking about a few nights."

"And what if they work? Then a few nights become nearly every night and then the depressants weaken his immune system further and he's susceptible to more infection, okay then, more antibiotics! Up, down, up down. He's got to live, in *his* body."

"He's suffering."

"No pill is going to change that."

Ruff! Salsa, awakened by the rising voices comes trotting across the kitchen toward Danny. Danny opens the door quickly and quietly only to shut it again loudly.

"Hey guys," he yells artificially, scratching Salsa's head with a clean thumb before heading to the kitchen.

Stepping quickly and completely unsubtly, Perry intercepts Danny at the end of the hall. Stooping, Perry tugs the dog's ear while speaking.

"Say sport, I didn't get a chance to walk Salsa, think you

could give her a quick eight blocks?"

To one side of his father is the living-room and his mother picking at the plants, to the other, the kitchen and a box labelled *Sleep-e-Dees* on the counter.

"I'll get you an apple," Perry adds as Danny returns to the door.

Looking back at the tossed apple in mid-air, Danny notices the counter swept clean.

"Not too long, dinner's just starting."

Staring down at the sizzling skillet, Rebecca stands as if split open, feeling like her ribs are cupboard doors hanging off her spine.

Coming in with the smell of fresh air all over him and seeing this familiar hunch in his mother's shoulders, Danny crosses another confused kitchen. Salsa the faithful trotter.

Rebecca works a hissing network of onions, taking the end of a metal spatula to a few extra-long pieces that escaped her chop. The spatula halves the onions imperfectly, leaving rough ends like improvised fishing worms.

She feels Danny leave the room without looking. There are numbers on his thigh—a convict of hives on the lam in her house. His fingers are bad but calm right now. When they're lit-up with itching he becomes a quick stranger. She can stand above him and yell every protest and still he digs each hand with the other, fingers peeling their neighbours. In the past she has pulled his wrists apart and stopped him with a square look to the eye. But not for some months now. Glancing through his books while cleaning up his room she has seen small yellow stains on the pages, circles and stripes from the ichor of his fingers.

Rebecca has also seen the magazines between his mattresses and been unable to avoid worrying what he'll do in a few years. How will he bury those fingers or stroke a young breast? She put the air-brushed idiots back where she found them and drove to the nearby *Kwik-E-Mart*, buying her first pack of cigarettes in seven years. Still in the parking-lot and fumbling with the cylindrical lighter she coughed in her beige car, pummelled by flashes of quick, glossy cunt.

The potatoes are nearly done. Perry and Danny are talking in front of the TV. He can stop Danny's scratching with two low words from the back of his throat. *Hey fella.* Or, Danny, *stop it.* It's the same intonation Salsa will never disobey. Rebecca hates the way he's mastered the two syllables, *Sal-sa.* Their dog.

The meal is hard and silent. Every fork-fall clangs up Rebecca's spine. She's relieved to get up for another bag of milk. It was just yesterday she'd been thinking of new plates again. Danny doesn't stay for ice-cream.

Silently removing the cold-pack from the freezer Danny heads up to his room. Sliding up his shorts he lays the cold, pliant plastic over the day's fading score, grabbing *Sword of Thieves* to pass the time. Cold to bring down the hives. Eventually he lays a dirty T-shirt between thigh and liquid ice. Then, after an hour, it's Rebecca's hairdryer.

Standing with the bathroom door closed (an emerging specialty of his) Danny sprays his thigh with hot air, massaging the surrounding skin with one hand. Cutting the heat he fishes in a pocket for the golf-pencil.

Pressing M O M firmly over the fading digits.

He tries the hairdryer all night, hoping to get a rise before morning.

Eventually Perry yells up curiously, the TV muted temporarily.

"Danny, everything okay up there?"

"Yeah Dad, just trying to get some glue to dry."

"What?"

"It's a surprise."

"Okay," and the TV floods again.

M O M doesn't come up that night, despite effort and heat.

Danny wakes late, his dad already gone and the sun shining for a dozen Julys. With crazy hair and the smell of sleep all over him, Danny hunts out his mother at the dining-room table. Bathrobe, newspaper and a mug of coffee.

Having thrown on just his shorts, Danny flinches slightly with the morning chill.

"Mom, look," Danny says, raising the *L'il Walkers* up his thigh.

M O M

His mother cries like he's never heard. Her chin goes to rubber and the tears stream onto her peach bathrobe. Sunshine swats at the dust and the steam keeps rising from Rebecca's coffee. Danny is thinking *old,* thinking *lonely.*

Kermit is Smut

It's Tuesday. Auster Rawls is 37 years old and high before breakfast. The 7:15 alarm, the 7:20 joint, the nine o'clock bell. Wednesday, Thursday, Friday.

Each morning he slips on his loose, almost-silk bathrobe and passes two vacant rooms before reaching the stairs, empty heat all around. His sandy hair, untied and thin with sleep, clings to his neck like a sweaty shirt.

Auster rolls and smokes at a dining-room table scarred by its first lawyer's bill, drinking from a tall glass of cold milk between puffs. A white cylinder in each hand, the milk eventually biting like cheese.

The dining-room walls are patient and unbearable. Santa Fe Sunset, a washed-out orange that seems to freeze each night and thaw all morning. The walls against which he would notice each new tint in Carol's hair, Copper Russet, or Blood on the Rocks. It's been eight days since he last saw Carol. She was wearing leather pants.

Waking 'n Baking means dawdling in his bathrobe that much longer. He hopes his six-year-old students won't recognize the smell of pot, but still, noses everywhere—the Grade 8 kids with leather jackets, the dog-eat-dog world of the staff-room and its fire-hydrant coffee urn. Sweet Mademoiselle Taylor just two doors down, smart olive jackets, long gauzy skirts and that smile that occasionally rises up and spills into the corner of her eyes.

The large, open house is pre-warmed by a programmable thermostat. Smoking over the table, the heat of the entire room becomes a loose sweater. Warm, scented and elsewhere, dress is his last concern. Auster is wearing ties again and his shave is becoming impeccable.

"The necktie," Carol has teased while standing inches from his chest doing him up in a half-Windsor, "the last vestige of male plumage."

"Kiss the pretty peacock."

Those days of tongue before class.

Auster locks the Colonial blue door behind him and pockets an almost lonely key. The warmth of the late September sun is non-committal, the whole sky gone lazy. Sliding a pair of large black headphones over his ears, Auster waves at complacent Mrs. Charn heading toward her Subaru.

The empty house is a block behind him, cooling obediently; Davis Street Exemplary Elementary just three more in front. Four trips a day, ears covered in music. *Auster you never listen!*

Carol always loved September, sweaters with shorts and socks, crisp apples and cool swims.

The Davis Street door shuts behind Auster as he lowers his headphones around his neck. Small voices fill the halls and Auster's blood charges. Stepping around a rampaging bowl-cut Auster avoids the open staff-room door, sensing a team of curious exorcist heads turning to follow his path.

Auster in his classroom kingdom: the back-corner desert of the sandbox, the plotting fiefdoms of the reading-groups, the magic-tapestry of the chalkboard. Time itself winks at Auster in the second before the bell. Each morning he raises his head and stares out the sly window at the snug houses and tame trees, a fighter before the bell, Houdini at the last padlock. *My moment, Carol.*

"Good morning class." He's Karl Marx feeling impish.

"Good morning Mr. Rawls." The daily purr in his ear.

The neatness of their skulls is amazing and each desk shimmers like a digital mirage. Auster is lit up, the dope throbbing sweetly. Turning his head from chalkboard to class, pupil to pupil, to the minute dunes of the sandbox, he feels his ponytail swish back and forth across his collar as his lips make shapes and his lungs spill sound.

"Who would like to start today's reading?"

A sheaf of hands rises swift and clean.

Class, Auster has still never begun, *we need to talk about love. Love reminds us life is a gamble we otherwise wouldn't make.*

Everyday he sees how small their teeth are.

"All right Jeremy, would you start us off with Mr. Muggs please?"

And where, pray tell, is Mrs. Muggs? Locked around some whimpering, mounted mongrel?

"Mr. Muggzz saw the boll."

More aplomb Jeremy, please. Feel the author's words.

Each child is obviously a reincarnation. Once-petty statesmen hold a monopoly on the building blocks. A yesterday booze-hag fidgets while furtively eyeing the nearest glue cache. Freud himself giggles in the back corner, ever chewing a pencil. Auster will return every wayward soul to literacy.

"Thank you...Jeremy."

Was that a gap? Did they notice? It was a gap—now you're gapping—

"Who's next?" *Hmm, Carol? Squash coach? Your whole freaking legal team?*

The classroom is heated by two large ceiling vents, heavy grey concentric circles in the discoloured, once-white tiles. Bats of heat drop from each grey circle, swooping through little Suzie Derken's angel-blond hair and breaking what Auster once thought of as his concentration.

"Suzie, give ol' Muggs a spin."

Auster is a certified Whole-Language Specialist.

Auster knows the Honeywell Lite Touch III better than a thirteen-year-old knows his parents' VCR. Synchronized with every clock in the house. Each feature exhaustively explored. Autumn Build. Spring Fade. The electronic thermostat faithfully warms and cools the house all day long, prompting his leave and welcoming his return like an omniscient, schematic dog.

The Honeywell is a fork in the Auster Rawls railway track.

He and Carol had been running through a familiar itinerary of Saturday morning errands, the hardware store fell between the coffee shop and dry-cleaners.

"No scapegoats for me, thanks," Carol added offhandedly, taking her bearings amidst lawn ornaments and discount barbecues.

Auster almost stumbled into a rack of eavestroughing. *Scapegoats?* Was their eight-year relationship really reaching critical mass in John's Do It Centre? Repulsion and lonely confusion flattened his eyes and muffled every sound. Carol was actually reaching for a computerized thermostat with one-touch controls while reducing his desire for kids, *their* kids, to his wanting excuses. Excuses to leave his stories half-finished, unmailed, or never started, to carrying five, okay, ten extra pounds, to never polishing up his French.

"This the one?" Carol asked, cocking a slim hip and holding up the Honeywell like the photo of any mugger in a police ID book.

Auster could see her large day-planner bulging in her handbag, her latest salon colour glowing under the shop fluorescents.

"Auster? ...Hel-lo, Auster?"

"Yeah, that's me."

"The thermostat. This it?"

"I'm afraid it is."

"Are you starting something here?"

"Perhaps you're ending something."

"Auster, sales, growth, mortgages. My customers aren't exactly going to just stand by for two years. Do I need to keep going?" Carol finished her question by handing him the thermostat.

Minutes later, joining her in their SAAB and sitting uneasily in the passenger seat, Auster realized Carol may never have had any intention of paying for the thermostat. He suddenly recalled his open wallet at each morning errand, his recent trips alone to the grocery store. Staring at himself in the side-view mirror he saw OBJECTS IN MIRROR MAY BE CLOSER THAN THEY APPEAR printed across his idiot chest.

A programmable thermostat for the mornings, the air warm around them when they awoke. Her Saturday morning breasts under the duvet, her soft Sunday thighs.

Outside again—wandering man. Auster still returns home for lunch. His marching feet obediently sound-off memories. Rushing from the school hoping to catch Carol between appointments, their simple chatter as they reheated two plates of pasta. The crispness of a certain white shirt and the blade of her décolletage.

To suddenly appear in the staff lunchroom would be too much of an admission. Look, poor lonely Auster—and egg-salad again?

Auster is convinced that listening to headphones makes life more spherical. This renewed passion for music is beginning to bear strange fruits of observation. The same pair of songs that keeps Auster occupied throughout the entire walk to school is little more than half-finished on his return. John Hiatt claims Auster is racing home.

Viewed from down-street the house looks too solid, edges sharpened all morning, windows turned to steel.

Shutting the sober, wooden door behind him Auster strides pointedly through the greeting of heat toward a tiny auburn box of artificially aged teak. The living-room stereo, also timed, releases Charlie Parker on pre-programmed command as Auster sinks into a black, Swedish easy chair.

Only a few weeks after they moved in Carol was off to a ten-day conference. For a week following her return she stubbed her toes and fumbled her hands over walls for light switches she could no longer remember. Auster would smile and put both hands on her hips.

The easiest thing would be rolling joints in advance, make a Sunday chore of it. He once thought that taking the time to roll each one would keep him in control, remind him that smoking is a decision. Working his fingers in cylinders and stooping for the lick, Auster's neck and shoulders feel vulnerable in the large empty house. Heat isn't magic enough for these ghosts. Parker himself is another demon. Sprightly saxophone chords flap through the fragrant air.

Auster bumps a stump of shame at the bottom of his full lungs. Carol prefers cash to custody of the house. Theirs has always been a relationship of spaces. The house she did not want.

Auster and Carol met over plastic glasses of sweet but free wine at a Get Acquainted Session in the Education Department Lounge. It was the mid-eighties and they were doing graduate degrees while their friends were making money by accident, taking bi-monthly ski trips and leasing European cars.

"Auster, isn't it?...." Carol asked with a lilt and one raised eyebrow just minutes after shaking his smooth hand. "I'm about to fight my way over to the box of wine, can I interest you in another glass of *Chateau Hier?*"

"For starters."

Through a combination of carefully hunted awards and scholarships, Auster could finally afford an apartment all to himself. After four undergraduate years of writing essays in the same room where he slept, dressed and occasionally got laid, Auster now had a desk and a decent reading chair outside his bedroom. Halfway through September Carol slid down on him in that favourite chair. They came and a wheel really did break off.

With an unspoken agreement that relieved both of them, the weeks became divided into separate working quarters and several nights over. Carol in a library carrel (and him with endless puns). Auster in his chilly-charming, farty-day apartment. As term picked up Carol would often work right through to the library's 11 PM close before dragging herself the few blocks to Auster's bed. Sometimes he would walk and meet her, sharpened by the fresh air, drunk by the fit of her held hand.

"The Whole Language System," he started again one night as they neared his building, "it feels like everything I've been waiting for."

"Any better idea of what you're going to do?"

They walked up the stale, brown stairwell to his apartment.

"Student journals, right there on the front lines."

"Get them writing and then start worrying about how they write?" Carol's mind liked to finish.

"Exactly, the animal wants to use language, not listen to instructions. I've been fantasizing—"

"—makes two of us," she interrupted, reaching in for his belly as he slid a key into the door.

"—about a book," he continued as they stumbled through his doorway. "Here, I'll show you."

"Big Boy."

Auster slid the pack off her back and dragged her over to his kitchen-table writing studio and an open textbook.

"Look at this," he began, pressing her legs into the table and wrapping around her from behind. "Years of writing with students and I'll compile a whole book of these mind-splitting misspellings."

"A Zen teacher's novel?"

"Have I mentioned your brilliance?"

Auster retreated as she glanced over the textbook's excerpts of teacher-student journals. Standing back diagonally he watched her read, a desperate chessboard bishop one move from the jump.

Kermit is smut.	Yes, Kermit is smart.
he reds.	What does he read?
he eat flyes.	Do you like to eat flies?

Carol looked up with questions but Auster spoke first, hanging on her eyes.

"Buckskin," he said quietly.

"O-kay—"

"The brown of your eyes is so soft, like buckskin."

Her sweater came up as easily as a clean sheet off a line.

Supper wasn't their meal. They were breakfast lovers, kissless fucking in the mornings followed by a full pot of coffee. Friday afternoons saw them bursting through his doorway with groceries, Portuguese wine and Carol's knapsack bulging with books, pyjamas and sweaters. His dresser creaked in protest as Carol's sweaters and underwear pushed for squatter's rights. She gave him her favourite shampoo as a Thanksgiving present, saying "Call it vested interest."

Perhaps he was rushing things at Christmas. Regrettably they were both pulling off to strained family relations in other parts of the country. They adopted a date for Christmas, had cheap champagne with orange juice and traded excitement over impending presents. Carol gave him a beautiful, obviously too-expensive cardigan.

Placing a small, square parcel in her lap Auster leaned back as she unwrapped a series of paper. One box opened on another. He bit his lip for the vulnerable instant it took her to finally uncover the small jeweller's box.

"Auster," she said before opening it, eyes swelling a little. She nervously tucked a wayward lock of unwashed hair behind her ear before prying the lid. Her chin caught slightly before she howled with laughter. Sitting on the purple velvet designed to hold an engagement ring lay a single, gleaming key. Carol's own key to his apartment sat freshly cut and finished with a radioactively tacky artificial gold plating. Reaching for him and smiling, all kisses.

Chuckling, they knew he was just checking. A key masquerading as a ring, teaching small children to read: practicing Carol, practicing.

The finish on the key wore off quickly with frequent use and the cardigan now hangs in Carol's deserted once-office, the only object in one of Auster's two empty rooms.

Rising from the chair's Swedish embrace, Auster swims to the kitchen, turning up Parker as he passes. Midday sunlight bats at the blue smoke. The answering-machine light flickers self-importantly in a corner. *Auster, just sign the papers.*

Up in the kitchen, the heavens, and the clouds Auster slices a bagel and races alongside a bullet-train of epiphanies. He isn't cooking much any more—just the grabbables, breads, tomatoes and cheeses, fruit and granola all day long.

What remains of his lunch hour is as much a pattern as its beginning. Sitting Swedish in front of the speakers, Auster nibbles from a plate in his lap and thumbs through a student's journal.

Naive Cormac Evans:

Suzyz Swing	Suzie's Swing
furst we cut abord	First you cut the board
and then the rop	and then the rope.
Suzys dad climd the tree	Suzie's Dad climbed the tree
on a latter.	on a ladder
He tyedt four Suzynme	He was nice to tie it for
	you and Suzie

Knots, Cormac, watch their knots.

Auster scans through the pile of workbooks, looking over the colours and names like pharmacy pills. Julie Phillips for a little sunshine. Sardonic Tommy Banks to take the edge off. Confiding Gabriel Rhodes:

My sistr is stooped and	My sister is also stupid
men	and mean.
She taks my thingz	She always takes my things.
that she wantz	She wants.
I hat her	I hate mine too.

Shutting down, the stereo timer strangles the saxophone in an instant and Auster packs up, brushing his teeth on the way out the door. Cool down House. Good Boy. His headphones are on and giving before the key is in the door.

A few steps from the house Auster turns and stares it down. Glenn Gould goads him on in each archipelago ear. The second-storey windows: bedroom, Carol's office, study-cum-baby's room. Auster picks up a roadside rock and hurls it at her once-office. The rock plunks off the siding as he knew it would. Admitting to purposefully missing the glass feels humiliating.

Turning, walking, Auster thinks of repainting her office for the forty-seventh time and hates every puppy. On Saturdays he often goes out for paint swatches. Burnt Umber, Southern Cappuccino, Midnight Vanilla. He had been planning on giving her a beagle for Christmas. Practicing.

Auster sits at the front of the classroom in the fortress of his desk, pretending to mark while trying to shoo away his stalwart erection. Staring out the huge windows his eyes land again on the backyard of the small split-level three doors from the school gates. A woman hangs coloured laundry on a bowing line. Plastic toys litter her grass.

The bulge in Auster's gabardines isn't going anywhere.

Without getting up he slides his suit-jacket on from the chair-back and reaches for the largest file-folder he can find. Covering the tent in his trousers Auster heads for the door, muttering "keep reading" as he heads for the Staff Men's Room.

Trust your dick. Believe in blood. She says you lack confidence. There are no kids.

Carol hides in the back of his hand, the outside arc of her right breast, the memory of her snail.

The stall walls are just a few inches taller than Auster's head. His jacket and zipper prefer to be open. A working hand swats the point of his tie, occasionally hitting the single key resting in his pocket.

The bubble-gum worms of his brain will always reach for Carol. Carol naked as he walks in the door. Taking off his jacket, dropping his pants into a rumpled, ankle puddle. Hanging from his tie as she takes him in her mouth, swatting his hands away from her jazzy hair. Tugging his tie, pulling him down to his knees. Sliding the loosened tie off his head and around hers, dangling it between glowing breasts. Turning, she slides the tie into her mouth and tosses it back over a silk shoulder. His hand on the tie, the bit in her mouth.

A mushroom-cloud of jizz fills the handful of crumpled toilet paper. The room and his morality settle back around him. The fading dope crackles distantly.

Zip. Flush.

"Jeremy, put the sand down."

Jeremy lowers the sand and returns to his desk. Another university-tower sniper nipped in the bud.

Marie, stop looking at my pants. Just a bit of lunch, that's all.

It's almost 2.30. The kids are restless for recess and he knows Air Auster is losing altitude fast. The soon-to-ring bell is becoming more and more Orwellian. The intercom is obviously designed by the KGB.

The recess bell rings and Auster's bones crunch. Stepping through the traffic he heads for the pay phone.

University had felt like a giant bow string being pulled back for six years. Then marriage, jobs, a house, the arrow flew for several more. He thought it all so easy, lucky. Walking to work, saving money. Carol working from home, also saving. A few years and she'd be into an office and they'd have more room for a baby. Auster has the room, empty, the paint too cold, the house silent. They were *married*, he had been thinking long-term, *life*-term. Weren't these plans just obvious? Reaching for a certain paint swatch or arriving home to the stereo already playing often catches Auster admitting that he was sweet but wrong. *Marriage means*, presumption if he's ever heard it.

"Charles good man, happy afternoon," Auster begins on the hall payphone, tucking a calling-card back into his wallet, "and how was Oz?"

Oz. Ounce. Ooh-zee. One ounce of hydroponic, herma-phroditic pot.

Carol has called Auster simple-minded despite his intelligence. Auster has a friend who smokes dope. Auster gets dumped. Ring-ring. Auster gets dope. Simple. Minded.

Walking back to class Auster tries not to think of why he didn't wait and phone from home. Threading his way through the toadstool desks, the walls of their distant house flare up on his skin like scabs. The whole shape is starting to feel rotten.

The kids file in.

Like most days, this one ends with Auster reading aloud. Taking up a book he sets the paint-swatch bookmark aside and imagines cracking entirely right here in this seat. He tries to let the words bloom in his mouth like instant flowers, remembering all the while where the wild things are.

The door opens and the heat is there. The stereo snaps to attention, letting Bird out of his cage. Now he understands

Carol's love of computers, systems, and stable principles.

It's not as if he's going to smoke away the rest of his life, just a few bags to get him through the divorce. If he's been misplacing himself for this long he needs a little external stimulation. Just needs to relax. Hates being alone. Work will get him through, Freud was on the money there. The dope allows him to relax and work at the same time.

Cutting another bagel, Auster thinks of getting away next summer, really away. This same knife has rested in Carol's hands, the very point of accusation. Auster had just returned from a weekend with Charles. She had stayed behind, working.

They were cleaning the kitchen on a Sunday night.

"Their kids have really changed their lives, I think that's exciting," Auster responded as he bent down with the dustpan.

"So long as you find being twenty pounds overweight, unaccomplished and high half the time exciting," Carol responded, scraping the stove-top with a cloth wrapped around a knife.

"Hey," Auster tried, "are you all right?"

"Me?" Carol suspended her knife strokes and fixed him with a quick stare. "Not loving mediocrity is somehow a problem?"

"Excuse me?"

"Forget it," she said, turning her attention back to a stubborn carbon puddle, "Did you finish the bathroom?"

"Gleaming."

Auster thought *he* was walking off until he saw her fading back reflected in the chrome of the kettle and realized what a strange monopoly she had on exits. Auster stepped outside.

Typically, Auster doesn't look at the stars often enough. Their walks ended long ago. *Dinner* was now pencilled into her day book. The sex, when it happened, seemed either combative or perfunctory. Sitting on the driveway with his head against the car's bumper, Auster admitted to his thermostat scheme. If we had nicer sheets, we'd be together more. Silk pyjamas. Warmth in the mornings.

A distant red dot caught Auster's peripheral vision. Two houses down a huddle of boys were trying first cigarettes on their parents' back porch, coughing, joking. Just yesterday Charles had told Auster that our peripheral vision lets in more light, "That's how animals and basketball players survive." Auster wanted to lecture a son on the evils of smoking, tell a daughter about *pe-riph-er-al* vision and the stars.

Auster pulled the door shut behind him and clicked the deadbolt. They'd get by. Her work *is* stressful. Don't be selfish. Buy her a CD on Friday. Get that thermostat up and running next weekend. We've always loved the fall.

Auster has had enough of these memories. He slides his bagel under the broiler and makes a quick trip into the living-room for a little memory solvent. It's just the roach from lunch. And it'll make dinner taste better. Marijuana Sodium Glutamate. How about a pot of coffee and a look through those old stories? Where's that breakfast roach?

Soon there's much more smoke. Auster is through the remains of the day and moves on to some quick pipe and lighter work. He doesn't notice the blue wisps rising out of the oven until the second before the smoke detector goes off, just like the dream that unfolds toward the crucial phone call that is actually the blaring of your alarm clock.

Christ, he thinks, running for the oven. "Shit!" he screams, after forgetting to use an oven-mitt. His throbbing hand, smouldering bagel and wailing smoke detector climb over him like animal shelter kittens.

Back under the smoke detector Auster reaches for the nearest fan, a pink student notebook, waving it in one hand while blowing on the fingers of the other. Screams of trumpet music rise and fall as the smoke detector starts and stops. Auster slams the stereo's power button and storms to

126

open the front door. Smoke and heat file by.

Staring at the sacrificed bagel Auster confesses that knowing he's high is becoming as common a realization as knowing he isn't.

Auster needs to get to the source. The Honeywell is only a signpost. His burnt fingers are training. Just a little more pipe and lighter to bridge the gap. Smoking his way up the stairs Auster steps into Carol's office without any observations about the colour of the walls. Taking one, no two, more draws, Auster sets the pipe on a window-sill and slides the old cardigan off its wire hanger.

Descending two flights of stairs into the basement Auster slips the cardigan on in reverse, fully covering his arms and chest like a plutonium worker in wool.

Kicking aside the few boxes of their things that block the furnace door, Auster pulls the chain switch on a bare, dusty lightbulb. The furnace, the tall blue heart of the house. Auster reaches out, wrapping his long, woollen arms around the hot furnace, closing the embrace with cheek against metal. Wincing, pain flying in and out of his skin.

To Take a Man on the Hill

When Edward Splintz first read Donne's line *No man is an island,* he had a full head of hair and a shit-hot mile. April 1997, however, finds him with a generous stomach, a newspaper in hand and possibly his last rotten idea. For a moment he debates cutting the article out or simply leaving the paper folded demonstratively on the dining-room table. Ed contemplates picking the boys up from school so he can share news of the race that much sooner.

Prince Edward Island is to be murdered with a foot race. In just 30 days the Confederation Bridge will be opened with a one-time chance to run its thirteen-kilometre distance. Linked forever to the New Brunswick mainland, Prince Edward is no longer an island. Geography is ending.

Caught with images of sparkling ocean and one long concrete track, Ed's never been more tempted to re-lace the old sneakers. He settles for a second fat Scotch before Cheryll or the boys return. Every few weeks Ed likes to forget the law, slip out of the office early and enjoy a few hours to himself in the house. He rarely comes across anything of interest but remains touched at once having found his track scrapbook under Kyle's bed.

Not having heard a car, Ed doesn't worry about his tumbler as the side-door opens audibly.

"How many of you?" Ed yells down the hall.

"Two and growing," Kyle yells back before Jason has a chance to respond.

Thuds fill the hall as laden knapsacks and behemoth sneakers drop to the floor.

"You guys eat?" a still unseen Ed asks of the noisy doorway.

"Zoning," Kyle responds, making his way into the house proper.

"Your mother's not back, you've got time."

The fridge-door opens and closes, glasses hit the counter and the gulping begins. Four nimble feet thump up the stairs in quick succession and Ed smiles while overhearing a slight skirmish over socks. Minutes later the boys are in the living-room stretching their legs while rock videos play in the corner. The sound of the screen-door shutting behind them sends Ed a little lower in his chair, momentarily uncertain about lineage and damnation.

Jason and Kyle pull themselves into the run. Four legs reach and lengthen. Two spines awaken.
"See her again today?"
"She's in my bio class, I see her everyday."
Generally they only chat while warming up. Each of them knows the wisdom of starting off slowly, plying the calves with oxygen, feeding the horses of their thighs. To race ahead prematurely is to jeopardize the entire run. But wisdom is often a drag. Nobody wants to be the slow man. Today it's Jason chomping at the bit. Kyle flexes like a bow.
Language has dropped from their mouths. Running is so simple—pain and pleasure teach patience. Hearts, lungs and legs pound toward that deep nirvana where pain and energy become one. On the great runs the whole body opens up. Kyle's arms have become wings—Jason's, fins. The bottom of each spine unlocks like a series of hidden rooms.

Safe in the knowledge that his tumbler rests innocuously rinsed in the dishwasher, Ed doesn't rise from his chair at the sound of Cheryll's car in the drive.
"Well love, how was it?"
"Oh," Cheryll yells from the hall, "home early?"
"Late meeting with a client, no sense going back."
Rendezvousing in the kitchen Ed simply smiles *hello* as Cheryll heads to the washroom. They'll each settle for a few

quick, ritualistic kisses when a slightly more relaxed and groomed Cheryll returns in a few minutes. Ed rummages through the cupboards.

"We still safe?" Cheryll asks, returning to Ed and a plate of cheese and crackers.

"Coast is clear. I do so love their running," Ed replies to Cheryll's inquisitive looks around the house, homing in for a kiss.

Cheryll still likes to talk as if they're the dick-in-hand young couple of ten years ago, the hiked-skirt bathroom feasters creeping their way around two young boys.

Breath claps the air. Four feet pour a tempo. Houses slip by—colourful, geometric scenery. Kyle is tired of these aluminum siding calibrations. His dreams occasionally take him to wheat, setting him, pace-perfect, running in the old prairie. Jason offers a quick wave to the ageing Mrs. Viyjha.

Kyle still hasn't asked if Jason too resents the home stretch. The growing sight of their mother's car often taunts Kyle with its familiarity. He wants to keep going. He isn't a practiced dog.

Cheryll proved most pragmatic about keeping the boys running together as their school lives accelerated. Having both boys in high school has created irregular academic and extracurricular schedules, throwing routines like running and supper out the window. September saw dropping blood sugars or cramped stomachs as one arrived home earlier than the other, starving and waiting for his brother with a snack. Empty stomachs mean short fuses and soon Cheryll was a reluctant spectator to sounds of stubbornness and hurled accusations.

Fine I'm going myself.

Ten more minutes and I won't feel so full.

A trip to the health food store and a steady resolve at the cash register returned Cheryll home with a box of athlete's power bars. *It's been a long time since the two of you squealed when not fed. Take one of these to school for afternoon break. Get along.*

"Hey Mom."

"Mom."

The two voices precede the boys' crash into the kitchen, glistening with sweat, panting and reaching for water. Kyle shoves Jason slightly in the back, a justified reminder not to hog the water pitcher.

Kyle is younger than Jason by just eighteen months. In school this has meant two grades between them, a distance far more significant than Kyle thinks warranted. Entering Grade 9 eight months ago, Kyle was outraged to witness Jason constantly afforded privileges both social and academic to which he was forbidden. As if Kyle wasn't old enough to go on ski trips. How is Jason really any more eligible to drive?

"Well?" Cheryll asks, unaware of her complicity.

"Twenty-nine, thirty-eight," Jason pants in reply. Six kilometres in twenty-nine minutes and thirty-eight seconds.

"Not bad at all boys," Ed adds while opening the fridge.

Jason and Kyle pound up the stairs to the shower while Cheryll and Ed prepare mammoth amounts of food.

Ed's been "showing his beer" for as long as Jason and Kyle can remember. When pressed, Ed generally defends himself by citing his devotion to the firm, the community (planning committee) and his early retirement, occasionally mumbling he'll work off his gut then. In his teens, though, Ed simply cut grace from the air.

Jason and Kyle used to periodically dig out the old black and white photographs of the lean stick in track shorts squinting under a crew cut. Even now old *Hills Bros.* coffee tins sit crammed with medals at the back of a basement cupboard. There had still been trophies on display when they were younger. Quite a speed, Ed set records at the scholastic, municipal and regional levels, often competing provincially. A specialist of the mile.

When the boys were smaller Ed bided his time.

"How far's a mile dad?"

"When you walk home from school, that's about a mile."

"How many miles is it from school to Grandma and Grandpa's?"

"Probably five."

"How do you tell?"

"You get used to it. On your bike, then driving. When I was young, older than you are now, I used to run track. The team practiced one mile each day." Really only Eddy and a few other keeners practised every day, and rarely just one mile.

At eleven and nine respectively, Jason and Kyle were already entering competitive track meets. If he was there, which he almost always was, Edward would linger on after the boys' races to "watch the older kids do the mile." On the rare occasions he did miss a race Ed would always end the dinner conversation with one last question about "some of the winning mile times." Each of the boys eventually asked about Ed's best time. The Splintz mile became legend with just three or four tellings.

4:32.6. At eighteen, Eddie chased angels. Second in the province, the best he'd ever do. He was personally invited to join several university teams for the following year. Each of these inviting coaches spoke of what a "fine boy" young Eddy was. But Ed knew where he stood. Telling himself that he would never win a national competition, never go on to the Olympics, he left his cleats in the closet when he moved off to school. At nineteen, part of him was already resigned to past glories. One mile in four and a half minutes, Ed wanted to be solely that creature.

Cheryll is surrounded by appetites—always this circle of hungry men. Amazed, she watches the dinner-table assembly line of arms endlessly driving fork or spoon. At least Edward clears his mouth to speak.

"Hear about the bridge race?"

"Where?" both boys reply.

"Think bridge."

"Mactaquac?"

"PEI?!" Jason asks hotly.

"What?" Kyle demands at the slightest affirmative nod of Ed's chin.

"13K. End of the month."

"How'd you find out?"

"How do we register?"

"There isn't a minimum age requirement, is there?" Kyle wants to know.

Older, Jason has always been faster. Wild running is part of any childhood and naturally the boys had their share of spontaneous races. To the stop-sign. Around the block. False start, you cheated.

Quickly enough Ed's boys were training, not just tearing down the street. Competing at eleven and nine, the boys started training three days a week by ages twelve and ten.

"Jaaa-ss, I'll be faster next time, I promise."

"No. You'll never be faster."

Cheryll and Ed had differed on this one, she suggesting that certainly Jason should slow down and train with Kyle. Ed remained firm through the days of growing debate. Kyle overheard a few of these exchanges. Jason didn't hide his annoyance at the prospect of any hindrance to his speed. Kyle changed.

If he was too slow to accompany Jason three runs a week, Kyle would run six until he was fast enough. And unlike a 40-year-old with a New Year's resolution, Kyle did it.

On Kyle's eleventh birthday, Jason ran alongside, beginning these years of regular, brotherly runs. No saint, and frankly a little less keen, Jason deigned to accompany his brother three days a week. Kyle continued to train six.

"Keep trying," Jason might taunt from the computer as Kyle laced up. "How slow?" he'd ask on Kyle's return.

Four lungs are smouldering. Nostrils bark air. Up until this month their route has been a steady six kilometres. The PEI race is thirteen. Air thick with each other's sweat. Their mother slid every rib, chambered each separate heart.

A dump truck hurls down this residential street, smothering the boys in a cloud of cloying diesel exhaust. Every lung invaded with exhaust, each bloodstream crimped with diesel poisons.

As a father and man Ed's a stand-up guy, genuinely liked by almost everyone with whom he has any serious interaction. The typical fortysomething professional, Ed is charmingly incompetent with his hands and generous but not flashy with a wealth which seems to have grown along with his stomach. At 43, Ed cried when Chester their retriever got hit by a car. Occasionally, when alone, driving home from the cottage solo at night or skipping an afternoon, Ed confesses to a blueprint of cruel egotism.

Kyle understands the mile, not because he's smarter, but because he's younger and families do carve certain vantage points. The Bridge Race is just a bit part.

Jason arrives home like a train-wreck. Heavy shoes are kicked into the closet. A knapsack drops to the floor and four long limbs drop onto the couch. One hand reaches for the TV remote while the fingers of the other rest in the top of his pants. On a commercial Jason cranes his neck to peer into the laundry-room, confirming Kyle's absence with a glance for his singlet and shorts. Huh, only six days to PEI.

Standing in front of the fridge drinking from the milk pitcher Jason easily recalls Kyle here doing the same or reaching for the water after a run. Kyle sheathed in sweat, silent, a watch already reset to a bank of zeroes revealed as he moves glass to mouth.

Jason returns a stack of cookies to the bag, suddenly aware of how Kyle mumbles whenever questioned about his time on a solo run. As children it had been Kyle who put an end to discussions of Ed's mile. *Give it up. Ancient history.* The inside of Jason's mouth becomes raw chicken against his tongue. A white balloon of milk fills his stomach.

Having burst from the house in an explosion of flopping sneakers, flapping laces and a loose jersey, Jason tells himself that bending to tie his shoes will provide stretch enough for his unprepared muscles. Starting off, he is tortured by flashes of the distinct metronome of his brother's legs and his watch set full of zeroes.

Alone, Kyle races pain itself. His feet devour block after block. Shoes striking light and clean.

Jason cannot clear his mind. The limbs feel mutinous, his stomach a millstone. Kyle's legs are a pair of scissors. Jason is being snipped to pieces.

Kyle has not been running with Jason to make himself faster. Kyle runs with Jason to slow him down.

Duped, Jason scrambles through a reverse of their usual route, the slow lion in the pride.

4:32.6. Ed's mile. 4:32.6. Kyle's mantra. No longer numbers but sounds. Four. Thirty-two. Six. Five beats. For years Kyle wished for a four-beat time. 4:32 would be an easier tempo, amateur music. But the five have made him strong, a master of ungainly melody. A deep pelt of fur counts out a beat for each foot. The left-right samsara.

Starting at what is normally their route's end, Jason realizes this is the entire problem. He is trying to run into his brother. Their father. Houses and trees slip by Jason as he stares into the slowly changing distance in front of him, waiting for his brother to emerge like the suddenly arriving image of a developing photograph.

A winged dot emerges in the distance, a low-flying bird of pace racing up the other side of the street. Kyle's stride is flexible and even, all flow. Jason cuts across the street.

Surprised, each of them realizes they have never seen the other run so clearly. Soles of shoes and tops of feet fire like pistons. The pull of each arm. Until now Jason knows he could have halted Kyle with just a nod of the head or one extended finger. The asphalt shares their feet and all intimacies are now counterfeit. Navels will collide.

Kyle smiles. "Wrong way—"

"—Don't."

Having successfully stopped Kyle in his lie Jason is unprepared when his brother runs past and continues on. "Kyle," Jason has to yell in unbrotherly ceremony. Each runner twists out of gear, turning to face his sweating brother and the miles he has already covered. Jason reaches for Kyle's wristwatch. Manic for the proof of these numbers, Jason's too-focused eyes don't see his brother's free hand shove into his chest.

Kyle halts his running-on-the-spot and stands with hands more than slightly raised. Jason hopes his breathing doesn't sound as laboured as it is. Two jaws clench for a moment as these similar muscles weigh potential ferocity. Each fist and nose assembled has met one another before. Squaring off now with pulses high and bodies ready, both share the sudden knowledge that now they could truly hurt one another. Ribs are in question.

Kyle restarts from the hips, resuming his run with one long uncoiling from heel to head. Jason watches the yellow bottoms of Kyle's sneakers recede into their neighbourhood, the underbellies of two fish swimming higher and higher above his head. Kyle turns at the next intersection, finishing off with a few hills.

Jason is cement, his run barbed wire.

"So boys," Ed begins between mouthfuls, "what's the verdict, you driving up Saturday morning or camping Friday night?"

"Just the morning," Jason answers quickly before leaving the dining-room for another bag of milk. Kyle works through his potatoes.

"This race," Cheryll adds, "is actually exciting. I'm sure it'll be just packed."

"Yeah," Kyle perks up, "radio says 2000 runners are already registered."

"Racing to an island—my," Cheryll continues.

"What are you hoping for?" Ed asks.

"—Fifty."

"—Low fifties."

Kyle and Jason share a reluctant glance at this simultaneity of speech, Jason wincing all the more at his vague-yet-slower desired time. It's been two days since the realization run and neither of them has broken silence. In fact Kyle has been uncertain of their race plans until this very dinner conversation. Before the other day's revelation they had planned on driving up to the race site and camping nearby but Kyle rightly assumed those plans had changed. Too uncomfortable to ask Jason about a Saturday itinerary, Kyle is again grateful for Ed. This new dam between brothers will not, cannot, last forever, but for the next four days Kyle will harbour no distraction.

"Morning, good," Cheryll offers, "we'll do you a big pasta meal Friday night."

The boys leave at four to make the 7 AM start call in Cape Jourimain. The drive into northeastern New Brunswick could have been pleasant. Jason assumes command of the as-of-yet uncontested stereo, fast-forwarding compulsively, changing tapes incessantly and occasionally doing percussion with his thumbs on the steering-wheel. Kyle feigns sleep or stares out at the passing stars, the crushing dawn.

A blind sun rises and a steady stream of cars begins taking shape. Speed is already an issue. Traffic slows as rural roads give way to minor highways, merging carloads of runners from every direction. Each carload feels like a frustrated Pavlovian Christmas morning. Months or perhaps years of training lie trapped under seatbelts and behind blinking taillights. Somewhere in the distance a bridge of virgin concrete joins two provinces, catches the first sun and begins its lifelong affair with the wind.

The pre-race operation feels well-intentioned but militaristic given its scope. Twenty-five hundred runners arrive by car at the Registration Site to pick up their numbers, toss belongings into a courier truck and pack into shuttle buses. Registrants form long alphabetical line-ups. Jason and Kyle have each brought a magazine for just such an occasion. The still-cold field smells of trampled clover and gasoline. Plastic tent flaps crumple and snap in the wind.

A fleet of jostling school buses ferry runners to the Race Start Area. The shore is unassuming, an otherwise dead-end that just happens to burst into concrete song. The $800-million Confederation Bridge contests the sky, bites its thumb at the wind and snubs the tide. Blazing white in its fresh cleanliness, the bridge confirms every rumour of its virginity. Yet even Kyle assumes the surface has already been repeatedly criss-crossed by investors and politicians. Months and even years later, following the story of the bridge through articles and later books, Jason will recall this as a race over top of three dead workmen.

As races go, 13.5 K is more than small potatoes. At nearly one-third of a marathon, BridgeRace '97 is definitely a challenge for the "mid-distance" crowd. But the opportunity to run between provinces has apparently tempted many from the "short-to-no distance crowd." The congregation looks like a market profile for Runner's Choice stores. Jason raises a thigh alongside blade-like veterans stretching the cables of their legs. Kyle has joined a faction of lonely fanatics running blazing warm-ups back and forth on a service trail.

The design of certain sneakers rivals that of the bridge itself and the high-tech crowd sip power drinks while programming their digital hearts. Die-hards in grey trackies and flayed shoes grunt and toughen themselves as if still running after-school laps for Coach Shopowitz. Already Jason prefers those with a sense of humour—the chiselled Beckett look-alike in the tuxedo T-shirt, the woman waving the small, stuffed pig.

Only the rare squint in someone's eye or the dangerous shoreline footing of a desperate photographer gives engineering its nod. East of the bridge, two ferries plough through their swan songs.

A loudspeaker hidden by the crowd begins to mumble. No-one deciphers the garbled message, but the noise itself marshals the runners into one large communal body. Those closest to the speaker obey barked commands and a pell-mell order rolls through the crowd's tight trunk and squat limbs like neurological commands travelling the body of a dinosaur. The boys make no pretense of moving toward one another in the crowd. Already separated by at least 100 contestants, Kyle squirms ahead of Jason, perhaps avoiding eye-contact, perhaps securing his lead. The day's tight schedule demands that runners still on the bridge after two hours will be picked up by a support vehicle. Jason has visions of an Animal Control truck on double-duty or gleeful Shriners putting golf-carts to the test.

The sky is cut repeatedly by two news helicopters sweeping for perfect footage. A few fishing boats bob on the distant water; spectators perhaps, or maybe mourners. A pistol shot cracks the air. The collective body jerks forward.

The two lanes of the bridge squeeze 2500 runners into a kilometre-long crush of limbs. Amazed at the crowd, Jason half-expects to find fresh bread, local leathers and live chickens, all the clichés of an Italian market. Kyle will later joke he felt like he was running for U2 tickets.

The event is so besieged by runners that buses will continue to arrive for the first half-hour of the race. Yellow doors will slide open as impatient runners sprint the aisle of the bus, down its few steps and directly into a race they have lost due to traffic.

Naturally the bridge starts with a hill. A two-hour *Iliad*, the concrete colossus of the bridge grapples the lengthy serpent of collected runners. Around Kilometre Four, staring at the crowded line ahead and listening to the panting chorus behind, Jason sees the race as the favourite clash of physicists and mythologists, an irresistible force meeting an immovable object. Each thought seems to end with another glance at Kyle's back.

The competing Islanders, those brave souls who boarded 5 AM ferries to New Brunswick to cross for the run home, have the advantage of anticipating the bridge's halfway hump. The entire sixth kilometre is a sharp rise and fall. Hearts begin pounding like old furnaces and all around strategic positions are lost and gained. The conversations around Kyle simply stop as the incline increases. No-one speculates aloud whether the hump is designed for increased strength, maximum clearance, or pure malice.

The hill awakens two fears in Jason. The distance between he and Kyle may be greater than assumed. Or Kyle may actually be accelerating up the hill. Jason squares his hips and pours forward. Lower on the half-kilometre hill than Kyle, Jason knows his distant brother has endured more of this burning in the thighs, this scraping of the lungs. Still Kyle pulls forward. The unnoticed ocean keeps sparkling.

The latter half of the run is wetter. Fatiguing, more and more runners arc toward the curbside water stations. The precious liquid which isn't swallowed, aspirated, or poured onto a scorching head is quickly spilled on the fresh pavement as dozens of paper cups hit the ground in a jerky drum beat. Every second kilometre offers a few metres respite from the high, clean odour of new sweat as spilled water mingles with new asphalt, forging the smell of fresh rain.

Jason and Kyle seem separated by magnetic fields. The distance between them refuses to change as time and terrain slip by. The latest signpost reads *8km* and pain introduces itself to each of Jason's organs like a visiting inspector from Head Office. Kyle's shins compact and extend like reluctant pumps.

At kilometre nine Jason discovers the ocean. Kilometre ten offers several epiphanies. Enervated by eleven and twelve—the downhill glide and its clear vista of Kyle's strong lead. Kyle has made a trophy of his brother's father, determined to be more than genes alone allow.

Admitting he has lost, will always lose, Jason is all too aware of the hammer-stroke of each heel, the self-inflicted smithy-work on his bones. Kyle will wait silently in the Finish Area. Kyle has become someone he wanted to be.

The traffic is amazing. The race is followed by what has been billed as the one-and-only chance for pedestrians to walk the bridge. Festival organizers hoped for 20,000 people and 65,000 will arrive throughout the day. Jason and Kyle don't speak in the Finish Area, each of them assuming an agreement to rendezvous at the distant car. Despite this communication blackout they both seem to share a disdain for the post-race carnival and head for the next available ferry.

A long line of the race-weary make their way to the ferry dock, sure to be its only passengers. Boarding the thick, diesel monster, surrounded by talkative runners, Jason can suddenly imagine shiploads of soldiers flooding the ports, cigarettes and banter, private horrors mingling with communal boredom. Just ten silent feet away, Kyle, too, talks with the cooling and stretching around him.

"I hear," Jason speaks up for the crowd, "rumours about

medals. Anybody know what that's about?"

"Commemorative medals for the first hundred finalists," a bearded man answers back. "He should know," the man continues, pointing to a smiling and affable passenger sitting between Kyle and Jason, "he came in second."

"Congratulations," Jason says automatically, reaching forward to offer a slightly awkward hand.

"Tony Matzer," the man replies, taking Jason's hand and appreciation.

"How long were you near the lead?"

"Oh from the start. Usually fourth for the first half."

"And then?"

"I won my ground on the hill. Second from there on in."

"The hill?" Jason asks incredulously, "That a habit of yours?"

"Kind of." A boy's smile widens beneath Tony's moustache.

The hill that Jason saw in the distance, the concrete blade cleaving runners and brothers.

The rawness of the land is disorienting. Fields, trees and shoreline. Overcrowded, underprepared, the suddenly busy ferry landing is in no shape to return the runners to their cars. Having parked in one field, been bused to an abrupt bridge and ferried to a previously unseen dock, few runners have any idea where their cars are. The line-ups for buses are already long and stagnant. Topographical rumours abound and logistical mutinies are hatched.

Restless, skeptical and misinformed, many runners join a cabal convinced the cars are parked only a few kilometres down the road. Factions split and soon a long line of independents start walking. Kyle joins the revolutionaries before Jason can hear a decent second opinion. Jason too takes to the pavement.

No-one can see more than wetlands and trees. A few runners have even turned back, retreating on hopes of an

eventual bus. A sparse group of passing cars suggest another ferry has arrived. Buses do eventually hurl past the
impatient caravan, empty on first sight, returning twenty
minutes later with a full load of the weary. Kyle jokes with
thin race veterans.

Fuck it, Jason vows, turning with an outstretched thumb
at the sound of every car. The walkers behind him initially
snicker at Jason's desperate hitch-hiking. Everyone wants a
lift and Jason is asking. Cars and buses stream by.

A gentleman pulls over. Jason sprints to the car, his
fastest speed ever. Driving past the revolutionaries, he tries
to keep from looking smug. Having just passed Kyle, Jason
can't resist the side-view mirror. Kyle actually halts in
surprise.

Jason hopes his little time-saver may just get them out. The
race over, the Registration Area is now beseiged by a
bumper-to-bumper line of would-be walkers. Registration
has become a nightmare of whining and miscommuni-
cation. Jason can do little more than cradle the brake all
the way to the parking-lot's wide exit, hoping to spot Kyle
should he arrive, planning on waiting on the roadside.
With just twenty more feet to go Jason spots his brother
and honks. Kyle fights the crowd and Jason gains a few
inches. The door Kyle reaches for is already unlocked.

"Christ," Kyle tries, settling into the seat.

Finally breaking through the crowd the boys shoot onto
the highway, accelerating quickly, each amazed at the un-
ending line of cars packed with would-be walkers.

Dissatisfied with local static, Kyle tries a different radio
station. Both jaws are still fixed and all eyes are forward. A
long curve ends in an absolute traffic jam. Each of them
mutters *Aww fuck* as the trail of bumpers and tail-lights
swings into view, their voices starting and stopping together, an accidental prelude to two surprised snorts and
the first of the family's affected grins.

LEONA THEIS has won a number of awards for her stories, which have been extensively published in literary magazines and broadcast over CBC radio. Writing fiction is only the latest stop in a serial career that has included waitressing, garment-factory work, library science, adult education and research. She now lives with her husband and son in Saskatoon, where she is completing a novel.

GABRIELLA GOLIGER lives in Ottawa. She won the Journey Prize in 1997, and was one of the three finalists in 1995. She has also won the 1993 *Prism International* short-fiction award. Her work has appeared in the *Journey Prize Anthology*, *Prism International*, *Canadian Forum*, *Parchment: Contemporary Canadian Jewish Writings* and in the anthology *Tide Lines: Stories of Change by Lesbians*.

DARRYL WHETTER has presented papers on both Canadian and American literature in Canada, the United States and France. His essays and interviews have appeared in *English Studies in Canada* and *Studies in Canadian Literature*. He is currently working on a novel, *No Friend of Time*, and a series of short stories about sex, mosquitoes, Iceland and profanity. He lives in Fredericton.

MAGGIE HELWIG was born in Liverpool, England and grew up in Kingston, Ontario. She edits an occasional litzine and has published one book of essays and five books of poetry, as well as two self-published chapbooks. She has also worked with a variety of peace and human-rights organizations in Canada and England. She now lives in Toronto with her partner Ken Simons and their daughter Simone Helwig.

Previous volumes in this series contained stories by the following writers:

1997: Elyse Gasco, Dennis Bock and Nadine McInnis
1996: Lewis DeSoto, Murray Logan and Kelley Aitken
1995: Warren Cariou, Marilyn Gear Pilling and François Bonneville
1994: Donald McNeill, Elise Levine and Lisa Moore
1993: Gayla Reid, Hannah Grant and Barbara Parkin
1992: Caroline Adderson, Marilyn Eisenstat and Marina Endicott
1991: Ellen McKeough, Robert Majzels and Patricia Seaman
1990: Peter Stockland, Sara McDonald and Steven Heighton
1989: Brian Burke, Michelle Heinemann and Jean Rysstad
1988: Christopher Fisher, Carol Anne Wien and Rick Hillis
1987: Charles Foran, Patricia Bradbury and Cynthia Holz
1986: Dayv James-French, Lesley Krueger and Rohinton Mistry
1985: Sheila Delany, Frances Itani and Judith Pond
1984: Diane Schoemperlen, Joan Fern Shaw and Michael Rawdon
1983: Sharon Butala, Bonnie Burnard and Sharon Sparling
1982: Barry Dempster, Don Dickinson and Dave Margoshes
1981: Peter Behrens, Linda Svendsen and Ernest Hekkanen
1980: Martin Avery, Isabel Huggan and Mike Mason

Most of these books are still available. Please inquire.